A WIN-WIN
PROPOSITION
CAT SCHIELD

Cat Schield has been reading and writing romance since school. Although she graduated from college with a BA in business, her idea of a perfect career was writing books. And now, after winning the Romance Writers of America 2010 Golden Heart Award for series contemporary romance, that dream has come true. Cat lives in Minnesota with her daughter, Emily, and their Burmese cat. When she's not writing sexy, romantic stories for Desire, she can be found sailing with friends on the St. Croix River, or in more exotic locales, like the Caribbean and Europe. She loves to hear from readers. Find her at www.catschield.com. Follow her on Twitter, @catschield.

One

Multi-colored lights winked at Sebastian Case, enticing him to come try his luck. He ignored the electronic clatter of slot machines as they chimed, beeped and sang of fortunes won and lost. Gambling didn't appeal to him. He believed in hard work and perseverance, not chance.

A couple in their sixties halted in front of him, forcing Sebastian to slow. The wife insisted the buffet was to their left. The husband assured her they'd missed the turn near the keno area. Both were wrong.

Before he could circle past, the woman spied him.

"There's someone who can help us." Her bright-red lips parted in a cheerful smile. "Hello…" She scrutinized his chest, where a name tag might be. "Young man. We love your hotel, but it's very confusing. Can you direct us to the buffet?"

She'd mistaken him for a hotel employee. Not surprising. He was probably the only person in the casino wearing a business suit who didn't work there.

"If you angle to the right, you'll see it." He pointed in the direction they needed to go.

"I told you." The woman shot her husband a smug look, dead wrong but taking credit anyway. "Thank you."

With a nod, Sebastian resumed walking toward the bank of elevators that would sweep him to his fifteenth-floor suite. Missy better be there. While he'd been on a conference call with their lawyers, going over last-minute changes to the contract for the purchase of Smythe Industries, she'd pulled a vanishing act. That had been almost six hours ago.

Concern buzzed. He'd left three messages on her voice mail and sent her four or five emails. Not a single response. Assistants didn't come any more efficient or reliable than Missy. Should he be worried that she'd gotten into trouble?

Noisy, crowded, chaotic Las Vegas lured tourists with over-the-top promises of adventure and spit them out with blurry memories and empty pockets. Had Missy fallen prey? Her small-town upbringing in west Texas couldn't have prepared her for such dangers. Was she somewhere in the maze of slot machines, pouring her paycheck into one? Or perhaps she'd left the hotel and been accosted on the street.

A cheer went up from the craps tables on his right. If his BlackBerry hadn't been set to vibrate, he never would have known he'd received an email. Slowing his pace, he pulled the handheld out of his coat pocket. Missy had finally responded. The two-word subject line stopped him cold.

My resignation.

He stared at the concise note in disbelief. Missy was quitting? Impossible.

His executive assistant had been with him for four years. They were a team. If she were unhappy, he'd know it.

Sebastian dialed Missy. After four rings he was directed to her voice mail.

"Call me."

Without waiting to see if she would, he shot her a terse text message demanding her location. Thirty seconds later, he received a response.

The bar.

Which bar?

He gnashed his teeth during an even longer pause.

Zador.

He pulled up a mental image of the casino's layout and turned to his left. A five-minute hike brought him to the bar. Red walls, black-lacquer accents and Asian-inspired art gave Sebastian the feeling he'd been transported halfway around the world. Enormous fish tanks lined the wall and provided most of the room's light. Twelve-inch koi drifted through the clear water as Sebastian strode into the room, scanning the occupied tables for his assistant. A redhead at the bar derailed his search.

She faced the bartender, gesturing as they conversed. With her back to him, Sebastian couldn't hear her laugh but suspected it would be husky and intimate, a siren sound that lured men into her sensual web. She sat with her long legs hitched to one side, her modest hemline offering a view of slender calves and delicate ankles.

Even without seeing her face, he was hooked.

Her allure was so potent he'd taken half a dozen steps in her direction before he recalled why he'd come here. A quick survey of the room assured him that Missy didn't occupy any of the small round tables. He would deal with her later.

First, he needed to meet the redhead at the bar.

"No, no. Really. He did that?"

Sebastian was close enough to recognize the redhead's voice. Shock vibrated through him. "Missy?"

His assistant turned her head and peered up at him through a screen of long, dark lashes. If it had been another woman, he would have described the action as flirtatious. But this was Missy.

"Hello, Sebastian." Her voice rasped along his nerves like nails dragged over bare skin. She pivoted the stool a quarter turn and gestured at the empty seat beside her. "Joe, get my boss a shot of Patrón."

Sebastian sank onto the stool, unable to believe what he was seeing.

Where were her glasses? Her eyes, the rich hazel of a mossy grotto, watched him with open curiosity, waiting for him to say or do something.

"What's with your email?" he demanded, struggling to pull free of the whirlpool of attraction he'd been sucked into. "You picked a hell of a time to quit."

She nudged the shot glass toward him. "There's never going to be a good time."

He swallowed the tequila without tasting it. The alcohol's burn was a mild discomfort compared to the inferno raging elsewhere in his body.

At some point in the six hours since they'd gotten off the plane, she'd freed her lush, auburn hair from its long thick braid and cut off twelve inches. The shorter style waved and cascaded over her shoulders like Chinese silk. Had it always been that vibrant and alive? His fingers itched to comb through the cinnamon ripples and wrap the long strands around his hands. He could almost feel the sensual caress against his skin.

His gaze traveled downward. She'd traded her amorphous pantsuits for a figure-hugging dress that framed and flaunted the creamy curves of her breasts. Had her skin always been this pale, this flawless? Or did it just appear that way in contrast to the black of the dress?

And speaking of skin. Had he ever seen her bare this much?

The Missy he knew was modest and reserved. The woman occupying the stool beside him reveled in her sensuality.

Sebastian shook his head. "What did you say?"

"I said it's your turn."

His turn. His turn to what?

The valley between her breasts called to him. He imagined plunging forward and burying his face in her cleavage. To arouse her with lips and tongue. To suck one nipple after another into his mouth until she wept for joy.

The intensity of the urge shocked him. He hauled a steadying breath into his lungs. Her seductive scent infiltrated his senses and fogged his brain.

"Sebastian?"

"What?" He wrenched his gaze from her stunning cleavage and blinked to refocus his thoughts.

"Is something wrong?" Her lips curved in a way both mysterious and feminine. As if she knew exactly what he was thinking. And liked it.

What had happened to the levelheaded, professional girl he'd come to rely on these last four years? Maybe bringing her to Las Vegas hadn't been such a good idea.

"No. I'm fine." What the hell was wrong with him? He couldn't seem to think straight. He peered at the empty shot glass. Had he been drugged? "What were we talking about?"

"My resignation."

Her words slapped him out of the sensual daze. His brain cleared. Heat receded. Or perhaps retreated was a better word.

"What do you want? More money. Or are you after a better title?"

"I want to get married. Have babies."

More shocking revelations. She'd always struck him as a career girl. His entire image of her consisted of the efficiency and dedication she exhibited within the walls of Case Consolidated Holdings' offices. Sure, it made sense that she'd have a personal life that involved friends and lovers, but it had never occurred to him that she did.

"You don't need to quit your job to do that."

"Oh, but I do."

"Are you trying to tell me I'm keeping you from getting married and having kids?"

"Yes." Her long lashes fell over whatever she didn't want him to read in her eyes.

"How?"

Sebastian signaled the bartender for another tequila, shaking his head when the man glanced at Missy's drink. How much alcohol had she consumed? Her clear gaze didn't suggest intoxication. But what else could explain her rash decision to resign?

"You keep me working late most nights," she began. "You call me at all hours to make changes in your travel arrangements or to pull together conference calls. How many times have I worked through the weekend making last-minute changes to whatever presentation I'd spent the entire week creating for you?"

Was she trying to say he expected too much? Maybe he'd come to rely on her more and more the longer they worked together, but he liked knowing he could call on her whenever and wherever he needed her help.

"You never take a break," she complained, finishing the last of her pink-tinged drink. "And you never give me one."

"I promise not to interfere with your weekends anymore."

"It's not just my weekends. It's making your doctor appointments and getting your car serviced. It's dealing with the contractors remodeling your house and choosing the tile, color scheme, fixtures. It's your house. You should be making those decisions."

They'd had this discussion before. "I respect your taste."

"I know, but decorating a house is something your wife should do."

"I don't have a wife."

"Not yet." She regarded him in obvious frustration. "Your mother said things are heating up between you and Kaitlyn Murray."

"I wouldn't say heating up."

Although it annoyed him that she and his mother had discussed his personal life, he had no right to complain. He'd been the first to step across the line when he'd made requests of Missy outside her duties as his executive assistant. It was just easier to have her take care of his needs both professionally and personally.

"You've been seeing her for six months," Missy continued. "Your mother said that's the longest you've dated anyone since..."

She trailed off.

Since his divorce six years earlier.

Sebastian wasn't opposed to remarrying. He might have done so years ago if his ex-wife hadn't trampled his ability to trust. Chandra's antics hadn't just dented his domestic side. She'd turned him into a remote bastard with no interest in developing romantic entanglements.

Unfortunately for the women in his life, he'd tended to focus his attention on something he could control—making money. Growing Case Consolidated Holdings.

"Okay. I won't ask you to do any more personal stuff." He would eliminate one excuse after another until she ran out of reasons to leave him. "Does that about cover it?"

Her hazel eyes became polished jasper. "Nothing you can say or do is going to change my mind, Sebastian. I'm quitting. Effective as soon as this week is over."

"You gave me a two-week notice."

"You can have four for all I care. I have at least that much vacation banked." She caught the bartender's eye and pointed to her drink.

"Don't you think you've had enough?"

He clasped her hand and lowered it. Contact with her skin had caused a startling revelation. He wanted her in ways that were primitive and defied rational thought. What was wrong with him? This was Missy. They'd worked side by side for four years with no sizzle, no fireworks. No craving to spend hours lost in sensual exploration.

She was his employee and as such, he was responsible for her. Only he wasn't thinking responsibly. He wasn't thinking at all. He was feeling. Hot. Intense. Sexual.

"You aren't my father," she said, sliding her hand free. "Stop telling me what to do."

He rubbed his thumb over his fingertips but couldn't eradicate the way her softness lingered on his senses. "This isn't like you."

"It isn't like the old me." She chugged half the drink the bartender set in front of her before continuing. "Do you know what today is?"

"April fifth. The leadership summit starts tomorrow evening." The annual week-long event brought together the executives of the dozen companies Case Consolidated Holdings owned. It was a chance to talk strategy for the future and facilitate a cohesive, global outlook among what were individually run companies.

"It's my birthday."

Sebastian winced. He'd forgotten again. Usually a card got passed around the office that he'd sign and there would be crepe paper and balloons decorating her desk to remind him to wish her a happy birthday. But he'd been preoccupied with the summit and the last-minute details for his motivational opening speech. What a poor leader he was if he couldn't even remember the birthday of the second most important woman in his life.

"Did I get you something nice?"

She threw her arms wide and gestured down her body. "A day of pampering in the spa and a total makeover."

"I have excellent taste," he said, his smile rueful. "You're the most beautiful woman in the bar." It probably wasn't the best comparison in the world because men occupied most of the chairs. The few women he noted were older and downright frumpy.

Her eyes narrowed. "Gee, thanks. Knowing that I'm hotter

than a bunch of grandmothers is a huge boost to my confidence."

Regret pinched him. He could do better than that. She deserved better from him. It was her birthday, after all. But the only way he could think of to show her how gorgeous she was involved taking her upstairs to his suite and peeling off her very sexy dress.

He took another kick to the groin. The residual ache made him frown. He was speeding down a dangerous path. Whatever had awakened a latent fire inside her, turning her into a seductress capable of ripping out a man's heart, was having a detrimental effect on his self-control.

"No, really," he assured her. "You look incredible."

"Incredible, incredible?" she demanded, seeking clarity as she often had to do with him. "Or incredible for thirty?"

Ah, a milestone number. No wonder she'd freaked out. She was facing another decade. That was especially difficult for a woman with a ticking clock.

"Incredible."

She pulled a face at him. "You probably think I'm overreacting to the whole turning-thirty thing." She paused so he could inject a comment, but Sebastian held his peace. "It's just that I always figured I'd get married at twenty-eight. Seemed perfect, you know? I'd have enough time for a career. Travel the world. Sow some wild oats. Make some mistakes."

He couldn't picture Missy doing any of those things. She liked going to movies. Knitted prayer shawls for her church. Rescued cats and fostered them out. If any woman seemed doomed to stay close to home and live a quiet life, it would be Missy.

But that was before she turned up tonight looking like sin, smelling like heaven, and tasting like…?

He leaned forward and brushed his lips across her cheek. Tasting like perfection.

She put her hand against her skin where he'd kissed her and regarded him warily. "What was that for?"

"Happy birthday."

Her eyes narrowed. "I hope you're still feeling warm and fuzzy when you see what I spent on my birthday present."

He shrugged. "You're worth it."

Missy's lips opened into a perfect O. How had he never noticed how sexy her mouth was before? With a thin, arched upper lip and a plump, delectable lower one, her cupid bow mouth practically demanded he smear her perfectly applied brick-red lipstick.

Without warning, her fist shot out and hit him hard on his arm. "Damn you, Sebastian Case. You can be such a jerk."

With that, she slipped off the stool and as soon as her shoes hit the patterned carpet, she was off. Rubbing the spot where she'd struck him, Sebastian stared after her in surprise. She had a hell of a punch for one so feminine. He launched himself off the stool as she neared the exit and tossed some bills on the bar before he raced after her.

She wasn't used to walking in four-inch heels so he caught up with her easily. Sliding his arm around her waist to offer her support as she stumbled, he murmured, "Where to?"

"I'm off to celebrate." She pushed his hand away from her hip.

Sebastian's palm tingled as he strode after her. He rubbed his hands together, trying to eliminate the uncomfortable buzzing sensation, and watched the way Missy's determined stride gave her curves a little bounce and jiggle.

His ex-wife had been model thin and forever on a diet. She'd lacked the one thing he'd always adored in a woman, generous handfuls of breasts. That might account for why he'd lost interest in sex with her. Or perhaps he'd grown tired of her neediness. Her lies about being pregnant every time he talked about leaving her.

Missy veered to the right as Sebastian was cataloging all

he things that had gone wrong in his marriage. A beat later,
e changed direction, stalking her down the row of gaming
ables. She moved with purpose, seeming to know exactly
where she was heading. He caught up to her at the roulette
wheel.

"Do you have any idea what you're doing?" he demanded,
ertain he already knew the answer.

"I know exactly what I'm doing." She pulled out a wad of
ash. "I came here to blow this and I'm not leaving until I do."

Missy had fallen in love with Las Vegas the second she'd
tepped into the hotel lobby this afternoon. The ringing slot
nachines reminded her of the final bell before summer va-
ation. Flashing lights and the prospect of a big win around
very corner unleashed her long-repressed wild child. She'd
barely resisted the urge to dash into the casino and plunk
own twenty dollars on the first blackjack table she came to.
n a heartbeat, fifteen years of sensible living went out the
window.

Sebastian set his hand on her arm and used his body to
block her view of the roulette table. "You don't want to play
his. It's one of the worst games for winning. Let's go play
blackjack. The odds are better."

His touch awakened a shiver despite the warmth of his
kin. He restrained her with gentleness, but Missy knew he
ould call on steel if he ran out of patience.

Rich. Powerful. Used to getting his way. Intimidating when
e didn't. A man in control of every aspect of his life. He
ever relaxed. Rarely smiled. Demanded excellence from ev-
rybody.

If she'd known what she was getting into before she'd
ccepted the position as his assistant, she probably would
ave run screaming from his office. Instead, she'd been drawn
o the mystique of Sebastian Case, the elusive, gorgeous, ex-
sperating millionaire businessman.

She shook off his grip. "I don't care."

"You've gone completely mad. How much do you have there?" He plucked the bills from her hand and riffled through them. His lips puckered in a silent whistle.

Afraid he might hold on to the money in some misguided attempt to save her from herself, she snatched the cash back. "It's enough to buy the wedding dress of my dreams."

If her use for the money surprised Sebastian, he didn't show it. "And how much is that?"

"Five thousand dollars."

"That's a lot of money to bring to Las Vegas." Concern deepened his voice into a dusky rumble.

Missy dodged eye contact, refusing to let his censure keep her from throwing caution to the wind. "It sure is. Took me two years to save it. I ate tuna sandwiches three days a week. never bought any clothes unless they were on clearance. I limited myself to one movie and one dinner out per pay period."

"Those are significant sacrifices," he said with a straight face, but mockery hovered in the back of his eyes.

Missy tossed her head. What did he know about making sacrifices? He'd paid eight hundred thousand dollars for a home because he liked the neighborhood, then tore down the house so that he could spend another two million building something to his exacting taste. A mansion he barely lived in because he spent so much time at the office.

"They were," she retorted, frustrated with everything in her life at the moment and taking it out on Sebastian because it was easier to blame him than face where she'd gone wrong. "Aren't you curious why I've decided to blow the money rather than buy the wedding dress of my dreams?"

"I'd love to know." Calm and measured, he sounded like a firefighter talking a crazy lady off the ledge. "Let's go somewhere quiet so you can tell me the whole story."

"I don't want to go somewhere quiet. My entire life has been quiet. I'm looking for a little excitement."

A chance to run wild.

Sebastian's disapproving frown would not steer her off course. She was tired of behaving like a mouse when what she wanted to do was roar like a tiger.

Daughter of a small-town pastor, she'd been a free-spirited kid, breaking rules and flaunting authority. True to herself but a disappointment to her father and mother, Missy's carefree days had come to an end in high school when her mother suffered a stroke. Bound to a wheelchair, needing help with the simplest of tasks, she'd needed Missy to grow up fast. Missy had shouldered a lot of her mother's daily caretaking until her death after Missy's twenty-fifth birthday.

"Haven't you had enough excitement for one day?" Sebastian asked. "You had a makeover. You've had too much to drink. Let me take you back to your hotel room. We have a big day tomorrow."

"I haven't even gotten started." She turned to the roulette table and plunked down her wad of cash. "Five thousand in chips, please."

Sebastian put a hand over the cash before the dealer could move. "Think about what you're doing here. That's a lot of money. Two years of saving and sacrificing."

She tugged at his wrist but might as well have been an ant trying to move a mountain. Her efforts brought her in close to his body. His heat surrounded her, seeped into far corners of her soul where wild impulses waited to be set free. His masculine aftershave invaded her nostrils and sped along her already overstimulated nerve endings. She was teetering on the edge of something reckless.

"I know what I'm doing." That was the furthest thing from the truth. She had no step-by-step plan. No clue if she was making good decisions. And she didn't care. For the first time in fifteen years, she was following her instincts wherever they led. Whatever the cost.

And it felt amazing.

"Miss?"

The dealer interrupted their argument and Missy shoved an elbow into Sebastian's ribs. With an oomph, he released her money.

"Five thousand in chips, please," she repeated, turning her shoulder away from her boss's frustrated frown.

His disapproval made her uncomfortable. As she had done with her father, she'd grown accustomed to doing things the way Sebastian wanted them done. How many times had she let his opinion dominate hers? Too many to count.

And old habits were hard to break.

The wheel spun before she placed her bet. Annoyed that she'd second-guessed herself, Missy drummed her fingers and waited for the ball to drop.

"Don't throw your money away like this," Sebastian said.

"Why not?" What good was being in Las Vegas if she couldn't do something that she'd regret even a little? "I was supposed to spend it on my wedding dress. That's not going to happen now."

"You'll find someone," Sebastian argued. "You'll get married."

"I had someone." He knew absolutely nothing about her, did he? "He dumped me." Yesterday. The day before her birthday. Two years after she thought she'd be getting married, she was back to square one. No. Worse than that, she was two years older with fewer single men to choose from.

"I'm sorry."

"You should be. It's your fault."

"My fault?" Usually he gazed at her in a neutral way as if he never truly saw her. At the moment he was assessing her with something other than his normal cool. "I don't see how."

What was going on here? Sebastian regarded her as if she were a luscious chocolate truffle he wanted to devour. Unsettled, she stammered her first word. "H-he broke up with me because I wouldn't quit working for you."

"Why would he care that you worked for me?"

Because he thinks I'm in love with you.

And, of course, she wasn't. Well, maybe she had been a little in the beginning. For the first year or so. But after Tim came along, she'd gotten over her feelings for her boss. Unrequited feelings. Feelings with no hope of ever being reciprocated.

She wasn't in Sebastian's league. He dated women with money and prestigious social status. She knew the type. For a time in high school, she'd dated a boy from the wealthiest family in town. She'd been as infatuated with his promises to take her out of west Texas as she'd been with the guy. But in the end, it was the sting of why he'd broken up with her and how he'd handled it that remained branded on her psyche.

"Tim hated how I went running whenever you called," Missy continued. "Every one of our fights was over you. I should've quit a long time ago."

"Why didn't you?"

In true Sebastian fashion, he arrowed straight to the heart of her dilemma. Her boss grasped underlying problems faster than anyone she'd ever known, including her father, who had an uncanny ability to read people. People, but not his daughter.

She couldn't answer his question. To do so would force her to admit that leaving his employ would be akin to chopping off her arm. She needed him in her life. Needed to be around him to feel alive.

How pathetic was that?

"I just did." Only not soon enough because yesterday Tim had told her he'd met the girl of his dreams, and they were getting married. Her hands shook. "I waited for two years for him to propose." Her throat tightened, blocking the next few words.

And he decided to marry someone else after only knowing her a month.

Tears dampened her eyes, but Missy blinked rapidly to make them go away. Facing her undesirability hurt too much. If she wasn't good enough for Tim, an unmotivated pharmaceutical salesman, who was she good enough for?

"Place your bets," the dealer called as people began setting chips all over the table.

Missy pushed all her chips onto red. "Five thousand dollars on red."

"Don't do this." Sebastian spoke softly but it was a command.

"Why not?" She didn't attempt to keep defiance out of her voice. He needed to realize she wasn't his to boss around anymore. "It isn't as if I have anything left to lose. Not really."

"Take the money and spend it on something of value. A new car. A down payment on a house. Something that will last longer than twenty seconds."

Solid advice, but she could never look at the thing she'd bought with the money and not see her wedding dress. The gorgeous flowing gown of satin and lace with the gathered skirt and beaded bodice. She'd cut the picture out of a bridal magazine two years ago when she and Tim had had their first conversation about the future.

"Tell you what," she began, feeling audacious and desirable beneath Sebastian's keen appraisal. Mad impulses had been driving her all day. Maybe turning thirty wasn't the worst thing that could have happened to her. Start a new decade with a new attitude. "I'll make you a bet."

Sebastian set his hands on his hips and looked resigned. "What sort of a bet?"

"Last call," the dealer announced.

Missy heard the wheel begin to spin and the ball start its journey around and around. From reading up on roulette, she knew she had a forty-seven percent chance of winning. Those weren't such bad odds.

"If the ball lands on black and I lose, I'll keep working for you." She gave a rueful smile. "I'll have to, won't I, because I'll be five thousand dollars poorer."

Sebastian's eyes locked with hers. The winds of change had begun to blow. Storm clouds loomed. Dangerous for the unwary.

"And if the ball lands on red?"

She licked her lips and his attention shifted to her mouth, lingering as if something fascinated him. Fever consumed the last of her hesitation. Every one of her senses came to life and soaked up the sights, smells and sounds of the man towering over her.

Hunger thrummed, longing to be sated. Only one man had the passion, sensuality and persistence to do just that.

She moved her left leg forward, bringing her thigh into contact with his. The effect on him was instantaneous. His nostrils flared. His entire body went perfectly still. His fist clenched where it rested against the table.

Intrigued, she shifted a few inches more. Her skirt rode up her thigh, baring more of her leg. She wore thigh-high stockings, the sort with a backing beneath the lace band at the top that allowed them to stay up on their own. Standing before the mirror in stockings and her brand-new black silk underwear earlier tonight, she'd been flushed with confidence in her sex appeal.

How many times had she watched his steely muscles flex beneath his tailored suits and wondered what it would be like to get her hands on all that unadulterated male beauty? To experience the immense power contained in his body.

Suddenly, she knew exactly how she wanted to celebrate her birthday.

His chiseled mouth flattened as she leaned into the space that separated them. Thick lashes hid his gaze from her, but a slight hitch in his breath told her he wasn't undisturbed by her nearness.

"I want a night with you." The proposition tasted like warm

honey against her lips. She had no idea where she'd found the boldness to voice it, but now that she had, she wouldn't take it back for a million dollars.

"I'm not going to take advantage of you like that."

A chuckle broke from her. Was he kidding? She was the one doing the advantage-taking here.

"One night," she coaxed, silencing the sensible voice in her head that howled in protest. One night to rediscover what made her happy. "That's all I want."

"This is ridiculous." Despite his words to the contrary, he didn't pull back.

Did he desire her? Was she brave enough to find out?

"Black, you get me," she said, hearing the ball slow. Only seconds now. Seconds that would change her life forever. "Red, I get you."

She slipped her fingers beneath the lapel of his suit coat and rested on the expensive cotton covering his broad chest. He grabbed her hand with his as her fingers grazed his nipple. His harsh exhalation thrilled her.

If something as mundane as standing close to him and touching his chest made her feel this incredible, what would happen when they were naked together? Her knees wobbled as his hand slipped around her waist.

His eyes burned into her. "Why are you doing this?"

"Because it's my birthday." *Because I've wanted you for four years but never dreamed that you'd want me in return.* "Because it's Vegas, baby," she crooned.

"Very well," he growled, arm tightening to draw her body against his. "It's a bet."

Two

The ball dropped into the slot.

It landed on red. Missy didn't need to look for herself or hear the dealer announce it. She just knew deep down that it was so.

And she knew because Sebastian stiffened.

In all sorts of interesting ways.

"Red thirty," the dealer said, confirming Missy's win.

She felt like cheering, but one look at Sebastian's tight expression told her he wouldn't appreciate her victory dance.

He loosened his grip, releasing her by slow increments. His fingertips grazed across her lower back just above the swell of her butt. Had he meant the caress? His remote expression offered no answer.

"I guess this means I won." She spoke quietly to hide the tremor in her voice.

"Five thousand dollars," Sebastian said, scooping up her winnings and depositing it in her hands.

"And you," she reminded him, clutching the chips to her suddenly tight chest.

Winning a man at the roulette table. If her family could

see her now. The thought made her shudder. She pushed aside her concerns. This was Vegas and everyone knew that what happened in Vegas, stayed in Vegas.

One night. One night she'd never forget. But only one night.

Her knees wobbled.

Sebastian scrutinized her expression. One eyebrow rose. "Let's cash it in and get out of here."

"Eager to start paying up?" Her weak attempt at teasing got lost in the cries of dismay around them as the ball dropped into place.

Sebastian caught her by the elbow and pulled her away from the roulette table. Was he afraid she was going to gamble away her winnings, or was he in a hurry to start their time together? The significance of the debt she was about to collect prompted an unexpected bout of vertigo.

Sebastian steadied her. "What's wrong?"

She, Missy Ward, unassuming girl from Crusade, west Texas, was about to sleep with the gorgeous and oh-so-elusive Sebastian Case.

If the girls in the office could see her now.

"My heels are a little higher than I'm used to and your legs are longer than mine." Missy tipped her head back so she could stare into his gray eyes. "However, I'm delighted you're so eager to get me alone."

His mouth tightened, but his gaze remained as impenetrable as reinforced steel. "That's not why I want to get out of here."

Four-inch heels couldn't begin to eliminate his height advantage, but she doubted even if they stood eye to eye that his presence would be any less intimidating. A born leader, he took charge in every circumstance. The perfect head of a family owned-and-run business where his brothers were strong-willed and opinionated.

Missy admired how he kept tension from erupting between his brothers Max and Nathan.

Cool. Calm. Collected. Always one hundred percent in control no matter what the situation.

The exact opposite of how she felt at the moment.

"Really?" She slipped on a half smile. "Because I was hoping you were planning on giving me my money's worth."

"Let's cash you out." Sebastian collected her winnings from her cupped hands and jerked his head toward the cashier. "Then we'll go upstairs and discuss this crazy wager of yours."

Not fair, damn it. She'd won him fair and square.

"We wouldn't be discussing it if you won," she grumbled as he turned away. She trailed after him. His powerful stride covered ground faster than she could in her heels. By the time she arrived at the cashier, she was out of breath. "You won't talk me out of it. In fact, the only topic up for discussion is what time you get to put your clothes back on tomorrow morning."

The woman behind the bars stopped counting out bills. She stared from Sebastian to Missy and back again before starting over.

"Keep your voice down."

"Why? No one cares." No one except him. "Unless, of course, you're ashamed of being seen with me."

"Don't be ridiculous."

"Then what's the problem?"

The look he leveled on her would have reduced every vice president at Case Consolidated Holdings to quivering idiots. Missy had seen it before. She straightened her spine and braced herself against his annoyance.

As the cashier placed ten thousand dollars in front of them, Missy counted along. By the time the woman had lined up the bills on the counter, Missy's lightheadedness had returned.

She'd won five thousand dollars. And a big hunky millionaire. She wasn't sure which one shocked her more.

Stuffing the bills into her purse, she tugged at Sebastian's sleeve. "Let's go."

She was glad to have him at her side as they found the elevators that would take them to the suite of rooms they shared. Besides having gotten lost twice today already, the wad of cash in her purse made her feel as if she had a target painted on her back. Knowing security was a scream away reassured her somewhat, but Sebastian's tall form guarding her body made her feel completely safe.

As the elevator rose to the fifteenth floor, Missy wasn't sure if it was Sebastian's ongoing disapproval that caused the panicky flutters in her stomach or the thought that within the next ten minutes she was going to be naked in his arms.

"You look nervous," he remarked smoothly as he slid the keycard out of his pocket.

"Nervous?" She released a wild cackle, loosening the death grip on her beaded clutch. Letting him believe she wasn't one hundred percent ready to make love would give him ammunition to shoot holes in her decision to collect on the bet. She cleared her throat. "Do I have a reason to be?"

A long-suffering sigh spilled from Sebastian. "You are obviously not the sort of girl who sleeps with a man once and walks away. Why don't I escort you back to your room and we can call it a night?"

"Because if you'd won, you'd collect, and that's what I'm going to do." She plucked the keycard from his hand and unlocked the door.

Sebastian's suite was three times the size of her one-bedroom condo back home and way better decorated. Latte-colored walls, carpet and furniture, espresso drapes and accents gave the room a sophisticated feel. Bold, modern paintings added slashes of color during the day. At night the Vegas strip glittered through the large west-facing windows.

The suite boasted three separate conversation areas and a conference room that seated ten.

While Sebastian strode around the room turning on lights as he went, she crossed to the wet bar. "I had them put a bottle of champagne in your fridge."

"Did you plan for us to drink it together?"

She jumped as he appeared beside her without warning. The carpet had muffled his steps. Eyes hard, he awaited her answer.

"It's my thirtieth birthday." Two champagne flutes sat beside the ice bucket on the bar. "I wanted to celebrate. I thought that maybe you'd have a drink with me. I don't know anyone else in Las Vegas."

"Did you order the champagne before or after you decided to resign?"

"Before." She'd been feeling blue this morning. Tim's reason for dumping her had opened a deep wound in her psyche. Stepping on to the plane, she'd felt like an ugly frumpy mess. Sebastian had treated her like a dictation machine the whole flight. She was invisible. Unremarkable. So when they'd arrived at the hotel, she'd bought a new dress, gotten her hair cut and styled, and realized she wasn't dull after all. "Can you open this?"

He took the champagne bottle and set it aside. "If you need liquid courage to go through with this, maybe we should forget the whole wager."

"No." She cursed her breathless tone. "It's my birthday. I want to celebrate."

She reached past him for the bottle, determined to open it herself. Shock waves buffeted her as he threaded his fingers through her hair.

His heat pounded against her like a rogue wave, catching her off balance. She grabbed at his forearms and hard muscle flexed beneath her touch.

He lowered his lips to the very corner of her mouth. Skin

tingling at the grazing contact, she shifted her head, but his lips were already gone. She sighed in dismay as he drifted kisses along her cheek.

"You smell like sweetness and sin," he murmured, dragging his thumb across her lower lip. "How do you manage it?"

Relieved to know he wasn't completely immune to her, she said. "New perfume. It's called Sweetness and Sin."

"Remind me to buy you a case for Christmas."

His hands cupped her head, holding her poised between close-enough-to-kiss and his-lips-weren't-going-anywhere-near-hers. Despite the anticipation humming through her body like a high-voltage power line, anxiety was beginning to seep in.

Why was he stalling?

Had she imagined the interest in his eyes? What if he didn't find her attractive after all?

Maybe if she gave him a little reminder why they were here, he'd remember his manners and make love to her.

"Sebastian," she began, her tone a low warning.

"Yes, Missy?"

In one long caress, he eased his hands down her spine to her hips and back up again. Her muscles melted against his hard body. As nice as it was being this close to him, proximity to so much raw male power was causing a dramatic spike in her sexual frustration.

"We had a deal."

"Deals are made to be broken."

"I won you fair and square," she said, determination punctuating each word. "So, quit stalling and pay up."

Frustrating woman.

Yet amusement dominated annoyance at his assistant's command. How had he never noticed her bossy streak before? "Where would you like me to start?"

"I'd like a kiss."

His attention zeroed in on her gorgeous mouth. At the moment, it was pursed like a disapproving librarian's. Far from kissable.

"Then what?"

His question launched her eyebrows toward her hairline. When her lips popped open to utter whatever brazen retort brimmed in her eyes, he lowered his head and took control of her mouth.

Warm. Sweet. Pliant. Her lips came alive beneath his. She opened to him and surrendered. He'd never dreamed it would be like this with her. No hesitation. No games. Just pure joy. Delicious perfection.

Right now, he wanted Missy like no other woman he'd ever known. His need gave her power and that infuriated him. But he couldn't stop the onslaught of longing to take everything she offered him.

Her tongue danced with his. Already he knew how she liked to be kissed and what to do with his lips and teeth that made her writhe against him in wild abandon. Desire swept over him, an enormous, overwhelming rush unlike anything he'd ever experienced. He swallowed her curves in his hands, pulling her tighter against his body.

Seconds before he lost himself, Sebastian tore his mouth from hers and twirled her around. Chest heaving, he trapped her in his arms.

"Why'd you stop?" she demanded.

Because taking advantage of this situation would come back to haunt him later. She wove her hips from side to side in a way that drove him half out of his mind. He groaned.

"What are you doing to me?" Fanning the fingers of one hand on her pelvis, he pulled her snug against his erection.

"If you don't know, maybe I'm not doing it right."

He set his mouth against her neck and sucked gently, marking her. "You're doing just fine."

"Do you need me to tell you what to do next?"

Damn her for making him smile. "No, I think I've got that covered."

He gathered her dress in his hands, bunching the material in slow increments. The hem crept up her thighs as she gulped in air. When her legs were exposed to the top of the stockings, Sebastian stopped what he was doing and grazed his fingertips along the very edge of the nylon a hairbreadth from her bare skin.

What was his ordinary assistant doing in clothing this provocative? "Sexy, sexy woman. You're driving me mad."

Missy murmured something unintelligible.

He didn't ask her to repeat it. Instead, he let his hands wander upward. Contact between his caressing fingertips and her bare skin threatened the semblance of control he'd recaptured.

"Sebastian."

Frustration filled every syllable of his name as it slipped from her lips. He sympathized. He ached for her in ways he'd never imagined. He drifted a light caress upward over the triangle of silk that covered her mound. Scarce inches below, her heat called.

"Are you sure about this, sweetheart?" He traced her panty's edge. His heart thundered against his ribs. "Because if I go any further, I won't be able to stop."

Truer words had never been spoken.

"Touch me," she begged, a catch in her voice.

Sebastian slid his fingers lower, aiming for the soft, wet center of her. Despite the throbbing in his groin, he stopped short of his goal. His muscles shook with effort while he forced himself to consider the consequences of what he was about to do. This was Missy. They'd worked together as professionals for four years. What if there was no going back from this? Where did that leave him? Leave them?

"Sebastian, please."

She squirmed in his grasp. His control wavered. He tried to hold on while rational thought melted as fast as an ice cube in hell.

Her palms came to rest against his thighs. The bite of her fingers against his legs sparked stars in his vision. Her frank sensuality excited him. So did her wanton gyrations.

"Sebastian." She seized his hand and pressed it against her hot flesh.

With a jubilant roar his carnal side broke free. Surrendering to instinct, Sebastian slipped his fingers between her thighs, applying the perfect amount of pressure to make her cry out. Satisfaction detonated inside him. He intended to make her come. He needed to take back the power she'd stolen with her sexy transformation.

She ascended fast. Faster than he'd anticipated. Great breaths turned her lungs into bellows as she neared the top. Her orgasm hit her so hard she almost took him with her. He'd never experienced anything as incredible as the feel of her as she abandoned all control to him and came apart in his arms.

To his dismay, Sebastian's knees lost strength. He knelt and supported Missy as she sagged, easing her to the floor. Once she was flat on her back, he followed her to the carpet, pressing her breasts beneath his chest. Linking their fingers, he set their joined hands beside her head and surveyed her flushed cheeks and unfocused gaze.

Mission accomplished. She looked as shell-shocked as a well-satisfied woman should.

Time to stop before either one of them did something they couldn't take back. He'd agreed to a night with her. No reason that night had to involve either of them naked and rolling around on Egyptian cotton sheets.

They could spend the time working.

That's what he should do. It's what logic told him to do. She might be disappointed, but she wouldn't be surprised. He always based actions on reason, not emotion.

Sebastian dipped his head and stroked his lips against hers. His heart rocked in his chest. What was he doing? This was madness.

He released her hands and framed her face with his fingers. She caressed his shoulders and gathered handfuls of his hair, tugging him closer. He obliged her with a second sweeping pass. This time, finding her lips parted, he lingered, tangling their breath, coasting his tongue along the inside of her lower lip.

She tasted delicious. Tart and sweet like lemons and cherries. Savoring her low hum of encouragement, Sebastian explored her teeth, noting a slight roughness on one in front. Her tongue flicked against his, and the insistent ache in his groin grew. He ignored it. This wasn't going any further.

Missy had other ideas.

He sank deeper into the kiss, losing himself in the heady wonder of it.

His world narrowed to her soft mouth and the passionate undulation of her body. Intoxicating noises erupted from her throat, their crescendo warning him she was on a fast track to another orgasm.

He might as well help.

Breaking off the kiss, he slid down her body. Her skirt had ridden up and exposed two inches of skin above her black stockings. He shoved the hem even higher, giving him a glimpse of black underwear. Silk. Tiny. And if that wasn't enough to enthrall him, the musky scent of her arousal invaded his nostrils. There was no turning back.

Sebastian placed a kiss on her skin just above the black material. She gasped. Intrigued, he drew his tongue from hipbone to hipbone and her body began to tremble. His mouth played over the fabric of her thong, teasing her with lips and teeth, down between her thighs to where moisture soaked the silk.

He smiled as he hooked his fingers around her panties and

tugged them downward. As she was slowly exposed to his gaze, he was forced to take a series of deep, steadying breaths.

She was a true redhead, he noted absently as he peeled the underwear over her thigh highs and heels and cast them aside. Then, settling back between her thighs, he leaned forward and with the tip of his tongue licked the seam where her inner leg and body came together. Her hips bucked.

Her wild, unrestrained movements made him want to forget the preliminaries and take her. But he held his own needs in check. He was the one setting the tone here. The one in charge.

By the end of the night she would learn what happened when she provoked him.

It was a mistake she would never make again.

He set his mouth against her. His first taste made him groan. Blood surged into his groin, drained from every other part of his body. He sucked hard and her hips jerked and twitched in helpless yearning. Using his tongue to tease and his teeth to tantalize, he brought her to the edge of orgasm twice, backing off each time until a low, keening sound emitted from her throat.

Then she did something unexpected.

Her hands had been busy in his hair, against his shoulders. Now, as he eased the pressure of his mouth and let her body quiet, she tugged her dress off her shoulders, exposing her black bra.

She snagged his hand and brought it to her neckline. Understanding what she wanted, he skimmed his fingertips against the rough lace before hooking them beneath the fabric. Her skin might look like cool porcelain, but heat raged below the surface of her breast, scorching his knuckles.

"Sebastian." The plea broke from her throat.

With ruthless urgency, he yanked the fabric downward, freeing her breasts. Large and round with erect rosy nipples. Every bit as perfect as he'd imagined they would be. He filled his hands with them, a savage groan rumbling in his throat as he settled his mouth against her once more.

Her every cry drove his desire higher. He threw finesse out the window and stormed her with everything he had. She shuddered against his mouth, her body taking her places he doubted she even knew existed.

She released a half-strangled shout. Sebastian pushed her still more and watched her climax unfold. Watched her unravel. It was a thing of beauty.

And he needed to be a part of it.

Fumbling his belt free with one hand while his other continued the movement that would extend her orgasm, he succeeded in getting his pants and boxers down far enough to free his erection. Harder than he ever remembered being in his entire life, he slid up her body and placed his tip at her entrance. Braced above her, he paused for a fraction of a second to ask himself what he was doing. Before the answer came, her hips lifted off the carpet, taking him in an inch. The silken caress smothered the voice of reason. He thrust forward. She was both tight and slick. The last pulses of her orgasm sucked him in.

The wonder that settled over her features matched the sensation expanding in his chest.

"Missy?" His fingertips grazed her cheek.

Her eyes flashed open, unfocused and dazed.

"Don't stop now," she whispered, depositing a clumsy kiss on his chin. "It was just getting good."

She wrapped arms and legs around his body, binding him to her as he began to move. A low growl of satisfaction rumbled out of him at the incredible slide of their bodies. They fit together as if she'd been fashioned for him alone. The sensation was beyond anything he'd ever felt before.

Pressure built in his groin no matter how he tried to hold it off. He wanted to savor the moment as long as possible. But her movements beneath him were impossible to resist and he drove furiously to his own finish. As with her, the orgasm hit him hard and without warning. Stars exploded behind his eyes as he emptied himself into her.

And collapsed, breathing hard, too spent to consider the consequences of what he'd just done.

Three

So that's what all the fuss was about.

Too exhausted to hold on any longer, Missy let her arms fall away from Sebastian's shoulders. He lay with his face buried in her neck. His chest pumped against hers as if he'd finished a mile-long sprint. She marveled at the feel of him buried inside her.

He filled her unlike any man she'd ever known. Of course, there'd only been two. Tim and her high school boyfriend, so she didn't have much to compare him to, but deep down where it counted, she knew that only one in ten million men could have done the things to her that he just had.

"Well, that was something," she said into the silence, her heart clenching in a manner that had nothing to do with her winded state. Repercussions swarmed her mind. She shoved the irksome thoughts away. She didn't want this moment to be tainted by regrets. What she did want was much less clear.

Sebastian had always been able to jumble her emotions. He could make her hungry for his approval and curse his pig-headedness in the space of one conversation. She craved his full attention but feared the effect it had on her hormones.

So, what did she want? An honest answer eluded her. Since she was fifteen, she'd let her family's expectations subjugate her heart's desires. Liberating her wants was as uncomfortable as standing from a crouch held for hours. Just as muscles and joints protested being used again after a long period of inactivity, so did her spirit.

Fear drove a spike of doubt into her chest. She closed her eyes until the pain eased. In her mind, she summoned every fantasy about Sebastian that she'd stockpiled during her four years of working for him. Was it reckless to want to explore a couple dozen?

Absolutely.

But if she couldn't check her inhibitions at the door in Vegas, where could she?

Her fingers itched to wander over Sebastian's back, shoulders, face, but he'd shuttered emotion and passion behind his granite features, and her earlier boldness was in short supply.

Glancing down his body, she stared, dumbfounded, at the erotic picture that greeted her. Her splayed legs cradled her oh-so-formal boss. The sight of him so intimately arrayed between her thighs, still mostly dressed, flooded her with satisfaction and possessiveness. He was hers. At least for tonight.

It thrilled her to have driven the impassive Sebastian Case to make love to her on the floor. He hadn't even gotten his pants all the way down. Or his coat off. She bet his tie was still perfectly knotted. The image of them with clothes askew in such a compromising position struck her funny bone. If her friends in the office could see them now. Few would believe that the decisive, controlled Sebastian Case could have gotten swept away by the moment. And not one would believe he would have done it with her.

He lifted his head, eyebrows hammering together as he stared at her mouth and the grin she couldn't control. "Did you plan this?"

"No."

Her wager had been desperate and mad. She'd never dreamed she'd win. Or that he'd actually honor the bet.

If she'd had any inkling, she would have stood at that roulette table, tongue-tied and as trapped by her family's expectations as ever. Even now, if she opened the door to her rational side even a crack, she'd start to hyperventilate at the stark reality of her and Sebastian together like this.

She waited for him to move, but nothing happened. Was he intending on staying like this all night? Not that she was complaining. Just thinking about it caused an immediate spike in her hormones. Tiny ripples of delight, aftershocks of that last incredible orgasm, tugged in her loins.

Chaos muddled her emotions. She cleared her throat. "So, what do we do now?"

For a long moment he stared down at her in that unfathomable way of his. Then, he seemed to arrive at some sort of decision. Tension seeped out of him. "What would you like to do?"

Her mouth opened, but nothing came out.

"You appear stumped." He eyed her. "Would you like me to offer some suggestions? I am at your disposal for the night."

Irony rode his tone. Missy chomped on her lower lip. Was that true? Did he intend to let her have her way with him? As if she could. He could snap her like a twig. Not that he would.

"You're frowning." He dusted his lips between her brows. "What's on your mind?"

His kiss relaxed her and increased her tension at the same time. Soothed her soul and awakened her desires.

"I don't have much experience with men like you," she admitted. "I'm not sure of my options."

"I see."

Was he laughing at her? Missy surveyed his expression. Neutral. No amusement crinkled the skin around his eyes or curved his lips.

She began again. "I mean, we've already done a couple

things…" She ran out of words about the same time she ran out of bravado.

"So we have."

"What would you suggest?"

Grabbing her by the hips, he rolled until she sat on him. "We have lots of things we could do next."

Where a second earlier she'd been exhausted, being on top inspired a rush of exhilaration. "Such as?"

His eyes burned with scarcely banked desire as he watched her. "There's quite a list."

"Starting with?"

"I could tell you." A second later he'd rolled her beneath him once again.

Breathless and lightheaded, she clutched at his shoulders while he dusted her chin, her eyes, her nose with his lips. The light kisses frustrated and aroused.

"Or?" She groaned as he framed her face with his hands and continued to ply her skin with gentle sweeps of his soft lips.

"Or." He drew the word out, nipping her neck, making her shudder. "I could show you."

His offer liberated her breath. It whooshed out of her. "Perfect. I love demonstrations."

Sebastian rested his forearm against the shower wall and his forehead on his arm. The effort it took to stand upright spoke to the rousing night of lovemaking he and Missy had shared. Cold water poured over his shoulders and back, deflating his morning erection. Waking with an ache below the belt wasn't unusual. The curvaceous Missy slumbering beside him was a different story.

The bedside clock had warned him it was eight in the morning. After the night he'd had, he was a little surprised he'd regained consciousness before noon.

To his intense dismay, he'd spooned Missy at some point

during the wee hours after they'd surrendered to exhaustion. Arm wrapped around her ridiculously tiny waist, face buried in her neck, he'd aligned them head to toe.

He'd never spooned a woman in his life.

Hell, aside from his ex-wife, he hadn't spent the night with more than a handful of women, and none since his divorce. He'd didn't like being touched while he slept.

Yet there he'd been, cuddled up against Missy as if he was afraid she'd steal away in the night. With a heavy, thick erection that poked at her backside. He'd kissed the side of her neck, his fingers gliding along her petal-soft skin. She'd stirred. Murmured. Stretched.

He'd jerked his hands away. The night was over. His debt paid. Awakening her with slow, sweet loving would imply that he intended to keep the affair going.

He'd been shocked by how hard it was to leave the bed. What was the matter with him? Sure, the sex had been incredible. Her enthusiastic, uninhibited responses to his lovemaking had blown his mind and unraveled his control. She'd denied him nothing. And he'd given her a night she'd never forget.

A night he'd never forget.

Sebastian shoved his head beneath the cold water to banish his steamy thoughts. Not being the sort of man who did things then lived to regret them later, he didn't like the sensation churning in his gut. He shouldn't have let himself agree to Missy's wager. If he hadn't been so damned certain he would win, he might have considered what would happen if he didn't.

What the hell had happened to his sanity? She was his assistant for heaven's sake.

Not anymore.

Losing the bet last night meant he would need to split his attention between the all-important leadership summit and convincing Missy to stay.

Everyone had a price. He just needed to figure out hers.

He slammed his fist against the tile. The sting restored his calm. He switched from cold to hot and soaped down.

The bed was empty when he left the bathroom to dress. His gaze slid over the rumpled covers. Images of last night's lovemaking flashed through his head. His body's predictable reaction infuriated him.

Convincing Missy they could go back to being boss and employee would be impossible if he let lust rule every time he thought about her.

Sebastian yanked a pair of boxers from the drawer and hauled them over his erection. Sliding into a shirt, he fastened the buttons and glared at his reflection, willing his body to behave as if he, and not it, was in control. At least Missy had made herself scarce. One glimpse of her sexy curves beneath the sheet and he'd have tossed his towel into the corner and his better judgment to the wind.

He found his watch on the nightstand and fastened it around his wrist before donning his suit coat. Sebastian closed his eyes briefly. Had he really been in such a hurry with Missy that he hadn't taken the time to do more than shove his pants to his knees? Obviously he needed to devote more time to his sex life.

Since divorcing Chandra, he'd grown way too suspicious of the women he dated. He treated every one as if they intended to get pregnant in an attempt to compel him to marry them. He and Kaitlyn had been seeing each other for several months and hadn't yet become intimate. So what had prompted him to throw caution to the wind with Missy?

Sebastian left the disturbing question unanswered and strode into the living room to retrieve his cell phone. The sight of Missy, wearing nothing more than a happy smile and the shirt she'd stripped off him last night, stopped him cold.

His shirt bared her long slender legs and tormented his imagination. With her moss-green eyes obscured by her glasses once again and her hair pulled into a ponytail, she looked like a cross between a pinup and the girl next door. What had happened to the conservative, somewhat frumpy assistant he knew and relied on?

"I ordered breakfast," she said, retrieving their clothes and shoes from the floor. "It should be here any second."

To keep from ogling her, he stared at the mixture of garments draped over her arm. "Have you seen my BlackBerry?"

"It was in your pocket." As she held it out to him, her neckline gaped.

She'd left the top two buttons undone, offering him a tantalizing glimpse of the voluptuous curve of her breast. His fingers twitched, muscles yearning to swallow that perfect roundness in his palm.

One night. That's all she'd demanded and all he'd intended to let her have. He needed to get them back on professional footing.

"Thanks." He watched her carry his suit into the bedroom, unable to tear his gaze away. When she disappeared from view, he shook his head to rearrange his thoughts.

He keyed up his emails to see what sort of trouble the morning had brought with it. Dueling emails from Nathan and Max told him it was business as usual with Case Consolidated Holdings.

A troublemaker from the moment he could crawl, middle-brother Max raced cars on the weekend and partied too much during the week. But as reckless as he could be in his personal life, he was conservative in business.

That made for some interesting battles with youngest brother, Nathan, who had made his money taking risks in the stock market and venture capital. The charm Nathan used to get what he wanted was in short supply whenever Max was around.

Max was in Germany trying to save one of their key suppliers from declaring bankruptcy while Nathan looked for a replacement supplier closer to home in Ohio. Max didn't believe Nathan's claim that the new company could produce their one-of-a-kind part at a seventeen percent reduction in cost and still maintain the quality.

"I have reports to go over from Nathan about this new supplier he found. I could use your help right after breakfast."

"I was planning on doing a little sightseeing this morning." Her voice emerged from the bedroom, tinged with impatience. "I've never been to Las Vegas before."

"There's not much to see. Just a bunch of casinos."

"That may be the case." She reappeared as a knock sounded on the suite's front door. "But I intend to win money in every single one."

The words on his handheld screen stopped making sense as she strolled past him. His gaze locked on her bare legs.

With an effort, he refocused on his emails. She would not distract him all week. Playtime was over.

A familiar voice greeted Missy at the door. Sebastian's head shot up. Framed in the doorway was not a room service waiter, but a tall man in his late sixties dressed casually in a golf shirt and khakis.

For about a millisecond Sebastian's father looked startled to be greeted by a half-naked woman, then a broad grin bloomed. The man standing just behind him, however, dressed like Sebastian in an expensive gray suit, appeared positively shocked.

The very air in the room stilled as if everyone had stopped breathing.

Missy was the first to move. "Hello, Brandon. Good to see you." She held out her hand to the former CEO and looked startled when Brandon not only took her hand, but also leaned forward to kiss her cheek. While Sebastian watched, she wrapped herself in professionalism as if she wore a business suit instead of a man's shirt. She then extended her hand to the second man. "I'm Missy Ward, Sebastian's assistant."

"Lucas Smythe."

Lucas might be seventy and happily married, but that didn't stop his gaze from roving downward over Missy's gaping neckline and bare legs.

"We've spoken on the phone." Missy's only sign of discomfort was the hot color in her cheeks as she stepped back from the door. "Won't you gentlemen come in?"

"Hello, Sebastian," Brandon called, noticing his son for the first time. "Look who I found in the lobby."

"Dad, what an unexpected surprise." And unwelcome. "Good to see you, Lucas."

Even more than getting caught with a half-naked Missy in his suite, the appearance of his father knocked Sebastian off balance. What the hell was he doing here? And with Lucas Smythe? Brandon had been against the purchase of Smythe Industries from the start. Not that he had a say in the way Case Consolidated Holdings was run since his retirement nine months ago. Still, this hadn't stopped him from popping into the office to say hello and lingering to voice his opinion of how his sons were running things.

Sebastian advanced past his assistant to shake hands with Lucas, making sure his body blocked Missy, giving her a chance to fade backward.

"Glad you could join us this week."

"Glad to be here," Lucas replied, his attention edging past Sebastian. "I'll admit I've been a bit curious how you run things. Want to make sure my company's going to be in good hands before I sign her over to you."

Strong in his opinions about professionalism in the workplace, Sebastian now looked like a hypocrite. The fact that Missy had quit before they'd had sex didn't make the situation any easier to stomach. Debaucher of female employees was not the image Sebastian wanted to portray.

"Have you eaten?" Sebastian asked as a waiter arrived,

pushing a cart loaded with covered dishes into the room. "Looks like there's plenty of food."

"I've already eaten," said Lucas, his gaze following Missy as she disappeared into a room Sebastian hadn't noticed yesterday.

They were sharing the suite?

Giving the appearance of being oblivious to the undercurrents in the room, Brandon followed the waiter. "I'll take a cup of coffee."

"Of course." Frustration engulfed Sebastian.

Uncharacteristically, he wanted to offer an explanation for Missy's presence in his suite and her attire, but his father's smirk and Lucas's frown told Sebastian they'd already formed opinions.

With ruthless determination, he banned Missy from his mind, slamming the door on his personal life so he could concentrate on the business at hand.

"Too bad you didn't bring your appetite." He began uncovering trays. "Looks like Missy ordered everything on the menu."

Brandon glanced toward the door she'd departed through. His lips formed a sly grin. "Have we caught you at a bad time?"

"Not at all."

Filling his plate with eggs, bacon, pancakes and toast, Sebastian sipped coffee and fixed his gaze on Lucas. Seeing the speculation in the man's eyes, Sebastian ground his teeth. He refused to feel guilty about what had happened in this suite last night, and he sure as hell wasn't going to make excuses for his behavior.

"I think you'll be impressed with the division executives you'll meet this week," Sebastian said. "We believe our employees are our most important assets."

"I'm sure he can tell that you appreciate your employees'

assets," Brandon said, stirring the pot with a heavy dose of irony.

Sebastian ignored the dig. His father had no business judging. Brandon had indulged in his own indiscretions in years past.

He turned to his father and decided to be blunt. "What are you doing here?"

"I told you. I came by to see if you could tear yourself away long enough for a round of golf."

"Not here in the suite," Sebastian countered, working hard to keep his tone even while nettles drove into his gut. "I mean in Las Vegas."

"This is your first time in charge of the leadership summit. With both your brothers putting out fires elsewhere, I thought you could use my help."

More likely he'd thought to take over the leadership summit and undermine Sebastian's authority as the current CEO of Case Consolidated Holdings. Brandon hadn't wanted to resign after his heart surgery nine months ago. He'd only agreed to step down to appease his wife of forty years.

"I appreciate the offer," Sebastian lied, regarding his father over the rim of his coffee cup. "But I have everything under control."

Missy closed the door between her room and Sebastian's suite and leaned back against it, heart pounding. Dismay tightened around her chest like a vise. She'd never seen Sebastian that angry before. Usually when irritated he froze someone in place. For the first six months she worked for him, she had heard one horror story after another of how he'd terrified her predecessors, and she waited for him to turn his icy disapproval on her. But he never had. Maybe because she made sure everything was done to his exacting specifications, giving him no reason to be annoyed with her.

But was that any way to live?

She deserved a job where she was appreciated for her talents.

Sebastian appreciates your talents.

At least she thought he did. He wasn't the most effusive boss she'd ever had. But he did give her a big raise every year.

But it wasn't enough.

She'd wanted more from a job than a paycheck.

She wanted more from Sebastian than employment.

Her nerves stretched taut as she closed her eyes and skimmed her hands over her body, sliding her fingertips along her naked thighs, cupping her breasts in her palms while she relived the highlights of the previous evening. How could she still ache for him after he'd satisfied her with hours and hours of the most creative lovemaking ever? She should be wrung out and exhausted—not revved up for more.

Missy pushed off the door and headed for the bathroom. Catching a glimpse of herself in the mirror, she regarded her reflection in bemusement. Her lips looked fuller than usual and felt more tender. She gently ran her tongue over her lower lip. Passion-bruised. Not surprising. The man could kiss. She'd been happy to let him demonstrate his prowess over and over.

Her red hair was a tangled mess. Her cheek color high. The neckline of Sebastian's shirt gaped, baring more than a little cleavage. She leaned forward to investigate the faint bruise on her neck put there by her boss. Branded. She stepped back and examined the full picture. Bare legs, mussed hair, well-kissed mouth. Son of a gun, she looked like she'd been up having sex all night.

No wonder Brandon had shot his son a knowing grin.

No wonder Lucas Smythe had scanned her up and down.

No wonder Sebastian appeared as if he'd very much like to throttle her.

He'd been in negotiations with the conservative business owner for four months over the purchase of Smythe Industries. Would Lucas Smythe reconsider selling his family-owned business after finding her almost naked in Sebastian's suite? Missy prayed that wouldn't happen. If her actions last night had blown the deal, Sebastian would never forgive her.

Caught in the undertow of repercussions, she doubled over, unable to breathe. What had she done?

Nothing any other red-blooded American girl wouldn't have.

Slowly, her lungs began to work again.

And really, what had she done? She'd slept with a man she'd known for four years. Big deal. She'd already quit working for him. No line had been crossed. It had been one night. Casual, maybe not forgettable, but certainly not life-changing. Sebastian wasn't interested in pursuing a relationship with her. And she didn't want to set herself up for heartbreak thinking she could fit into his world of money and social status.

For her, it had been rebound sex, pure and simple. After Tim's rejection, she'd needed a man to demonstrate that she was an attractive, desirable woman. Sebastian had done an admirable job. Her memories would keep her smiling for a long time to come.

Straightening, she stepped into the shower, taking her time beneath the spray. The idea of returning to the suite to face Sebastian's wrath lacked appeal. He needed some time to cool down. About a week might do it.

She'd go shopping. After her win last night, she had five thousand dollars burning a hole in her purse. The black dress had been her only new purchase yesterday. Sebastian and her father would counsel her to squirrel the money away. The pre-Las Vegas part of her agreed with their logic. Especially now that she'd quit her job. But her new future required a new attitude, and nothing boosted a woman's confidence like looking fabulous.

She stepped out of the shower, dried her hair, and then set about taming the natural wave with a straight iron. Humming her mother's favorite gospel song, Missy sorted through her luggage for something to wear. She'd packed nothing but boring business wear. Pantsuits in black and navy. Dress pants and sweater sets for sightseeing and business dinners.

Nothing sexy or eye-catching for her.

Tim wouldn't have approved of last night's dress. He was as conservative as her father. But Tim wasn't in her life anymore. He'd lost any right to an opinion on her wardrobe the second he'd met his "soul mate" and decided to marry her instead of Missy.

Piece by piece, she consigned her wardrobe to the wastebasket beneath the desk. The act of emptying her suitcase was no less cathartic than quitting her job or wagering five thousand dollars on one spin of the roulette wheel. She'd become too complacent in her life. No wonder Tim had found somebody new.

A firm knock sounded on the door that connected her room to the suite. Startled by the sudden noise, Missy answered it without considering her attire. Sebastian stood before her, holding her purse.

"Are your father and Lucas Smythe gone?" she asked.

"Were you hoping to offer them an encore?" His gaze burned hot enough to torch the towel she'd wrapped around her body.

An encore? As if she'd planned for his father and business associate to catch her half-dressed. Whatever had transpired after she'd left had turned his mood from bad to foul.

She glared at him. "Of course not. What is your dad doing in Las Vegas?"

"He didn't say."

"Did you ask?"

Sebastian communicated more with one raised eyebrow than most men could with a ten-minute rant. "He claims he's here to help with the leadership summit."

"But you don't believe him?"

"Let's just say I wasn't happy to see him in Lucas Smythe's company."

Few employees at Case Consolidated Holdings would know the vast chasm that existed between Sebastian and his father when it came to business strategy. Brandon liked to take risks and chase profits, often losing huge amounts of money in the process. Sebastian and Max preferred to use more structured methods when it came to growing Case Consolidated Holdings. Acquiring Lucas Smythe's company was a perfect example of where they differed.

The two brothers liked the conservatively run company and the way the acquisition would help diversify their mix of product offerings. Brandon wanted to spend their investment capital on something that might offer more growth potential, and he had an ally in his youngest son, Nathan. Problem was, to get to the big gains, it was often necessary to risk big losses.

"Do you think he wants to sabotage the deal with Smythe?"

"He hasn't had one good thing to say about the purchase. His showing up here means I have to keep an eye on him."

"What did you tell them about us?"

"Us?" he echoed softly, the warning hiss of a cobra. "I didn't tell them anything."

"Why not?"

"It's none of their business."

"But they're bound to wonder. The contracts aren't yet signed. What if Lucas decides not to sell you his company? You have to make some excuse why I was in your suite, wearing just your shirt."

"Like what?"

"You could have told him I'd gotten something on my dress and needed to rinse it out."

"That might have worked if you didn't look like a woman who's been thoroughly made love to."

She tingled all over, reacting not to his sarcastic tone, but to his choice of words. And his sizzling gaze. Her argument went numb.

"And the fact that we're sharing the suite." He crossed his arms over his chest. "Why are we sharing the suite, by the way?"

"We're not sharing the suite. My room adjoins yours. The door between us has a lock." That last bit sounded somewhat foolish. As if she didn't trust him. As if he couldn't persuade her to let him in. "You could have told them that I got drunk and quit. That I came on to you because I've had a thing for you for years."

His gaze rested heavily on her, weakening her knees.

"No."

"Don't be a…" She bit her lip before the rest of that sentence came out. Had she almost called the imposing Sebastian Case a fool? "What about the deal? Are you still going forward with the purchase of his company?"

"I don't know."

Her breath caught. She scrutinized Sebastian's impassive features, searching for anger, frustration, disappointment, but she saw nothing.

"What do you mean, you don't know?"

"Just that." His lashes lowered, giving him a sleepy look until you noticed the intensity of his watchful gray eyes.

"Yesterday, he was ready to sign the contract once one or two points were ironed out."

"Some things have come up since then."

"Like him thinking you make a habit out of seducing your employees?" Missy couldn't believe how angry she was at the moment. Angry with herself for lingering in Sebastian's suite because of some silly romantic hope that maybe last night had been the start of something. Angry with his father for showing up this morning with Lucas Smythe. But most of all, angry with Sebastian for his stubborn refusal to make explanations. "You need to tell him the truth. And if you don't, I will."

His fingers wrapped around her upper arms and bit deep. "Stay out of it."

Eyes blazing, he pulled her onto her toes and bent down until inches separated his mouth from hers. Memories of their night together swamped her. Her fingers loosened their grip on the towel, ready to discard it if he showed the slightest hint of wanting to pick up where they'd left off in the wee hours of the morning.

He must have read her thoughts because he lowered his head still farther. Missy closed her eyes in anticipation of his kiss. When it didn't come, she blinked in surprise. Sebastian had his own eyes closed. Tension pulled at his features, drawing his mouth into a grim line.

His chest lifted as he sucked in air. A second later she was free. Her heels hit the floor with a jarring thud that loosened her grip on the towel. It slipped off one breast before she caught it.

Snarling a curse through clenched teeth, Sebastian shifted his gaze to the pile of clothes spilling out of the trash. When his attention resettled on her, the only emotion he let her see was cool curiosity.

He used his chin to gesture toward her former wardrobe. "What's going on with you?"

"Nothing."

"You've thrown away your clothes."

"I don't need them anymore."

Iron-gray eyes swept down her body once again. "Planning on spending the entire week naked?"

"No."

He'd buried his mood beneath a neutral tone and an impassive expression, but her stomach muscles tightened. Getting caught half-dressed in Sebastian's suite meant their encounter was no longer a complete secret. Were they to be boss and assistant or secret lovers? She tingled in anticipation of the latter.

"I thought I would buy some new things," she continued.

He shook his head. "You don't have time to shop. I need you to go over the arrangements for tonight's cocktail party."

Missy's mood deflated. As far as Sebastian was concerned the night was over. He'd paid his debt. Time to get back to work.

"There's no need," she said. "I double-checked everything yesterday. We're good to go. Let's go down to the casino and have some fun."

"This is a business trip."

"And you can't mix business with pleasure?" She cocked her head.

"I've already done that," he retorted, biting off each word. The way he stared at her mouth, she could almost feel the firm pressure of his lips against hers. She swayed into the gap between them, brought up short by his next words. "Get dressed and let's go over the arrangements."

"I quit, remember?"

"You gave me your two-week notice," he said. "Time to get back to work."

He pivoted and left her staring at his retreating form. With a huff, she shut the door. She kicked at the pile of business attire that lay on the floor. At the thought of wearing any of it, a frustrated shriek built in her chest.

The phone on her nightstand rang. Summoned already? It had only been a minute since he'd left. She glanced at the door to Sebastian's suite and imagined him pacing. She understood his impatience. This was his first time leading the summit. In past years, his father had been the CEO of Case Consolidated Holdings. Since taking over, Sebastian had made numerous changes to the business that involved selling off two companies that hadn't fit their new business model and looking for new investments that were a better fit. He was growing into the CEO role and had a lot riding on this week in Vegas.

In the month leading up to the annual event, months of

planning had gone into every presentation, every speech. Months of hard work and not just by Sebastian. When he worked hard, so did she. Sixty-hour work weeks meant late nights and weekends.

No wonder her boyfriend had strayed. She was never around when Tim wanted to get together. A part of her didn't blame him for dumping her. She just wished he hadn't done it the day before her birthday and that it hadn't taken him less than a month to decide to marry someone else.

When the phone refused to stop ringing, Missy snatched up the handset.

"Missy? It's Susan." Sebastian's mother sounded unfazed by Missy's cranky greeting.

Over the years, Missy had grown close to Susan. And Brandon for that matter. They practically treated her like one of the family instead of Sebastian's employee.

"Because my husband insists on golfing today," Susan continued, "I wondered if you had any plans."

"Sebastian expects me to work."

Susan made a dismissive sound. "Tell him I need you to keep me company by the pool. I'm sure he'll give you some time off."

Missy ran that conversation in her head and didn't arrive at Susan's conclusion. "He really wants to make sure the conference goes smoothly."

"And with you behind the scenes, it will. Now, you've done enough. Grab your sunscreen and meet me by the pool. I'm not going to take no for an answer."

The people who thought the Case brothers got their determination from Brandon had never met Susan. "Sure. Give me ten minutes."

"Wonderful."

Feeling squashed between a rock and a hard place, Missy replaced the phone and scooped up her bathing suit. If she told Sebastian about his mom's request, she would be in for another argument. She dropped the towel and stepped into the suit. Sebastian was already accustomed to her flaky behavior on this trip. And it wasn't as if she hadn't already decided that she wanted to go have some fun. Susan had just given her the nudge she needed to act.

She slid the straps onto her shoulders and shot a last glance at the door to Sebastian's suite. Deserting her boss was going to make him even more irate than he already was.

Too bad.

Since starting as Sebastian's assistant, the only time she'd taken off was to visit her family. And there's no way anyone would consider that relaxing. Sebastian owed her four weeks of vacation. The least he could do is give her the morning to have some fun.

Grabbing her cover-up and a hat, she slipped out of her hotel room.

And when he caught her?

She'd cross that bridge when she came to it.

Besides, what's the worst he could do?

Fire her?

Four

Location?

Sebastian hit the send button on the text to Missy as the elevator doors opened. It had taken half an hour for him to figure out she'd pulled a vanishing act on him again. He'd intended to spend the morning going over his opening speech for the summit, catching up on emails and checking in with Max and Nathan. Instead, he was cruising through the casino, once again, in search of his wayward assistant.

His phone vibrated.

Pool.

Tucked into a protected hollow created by the hotel's tall towers, the pool area, with its waterfalls, swim-up bar and assorted potted palms, looked more like tropical paradise than a desert oasis. Two-thirds of the lounge chairs were occupied, but as it had the night before, his gaze went straight to Missy.

She wore a cerulean blue one-piece with a wide white band around the waist that drew attention to her hourglass shape. Barely a hint of cleavage showed above the suit's straight, unadorned neckline. In color and style, the suit was unremarkable. Sebastian doubted that anyone would give her a second look with so much skin being bared by the less modest women in her vicinity.

But she was all he was interested in.

His mother waved to him from the pool as he neared Missy's lounge chair. Missy looked up as his shadow fell across her.

"Are you sure you should be sitting in the sun with your skin?"

"Don't worry." She pointed to the sunscreen label. "It's SPF 75."

The morning sun poured over his head and shoulders, warming the charcoal wool suit he wore and raising his temperature. He tugged his tie loose and unfastened his shirt's top button. "Maybe you should move into the shade."

"I'm fine."

"With skin like yours you should be careful." His gaze trailed down her legs, following the movement of her hand as she smoothed lotion over her creamy skin.

His fingers balled into fists as memories of the night before intruded. The taste of her kisses. The way she'd moaned his name. How her breath caught as he slid deep inside her. The fact that her hunger for him had matched his need for her.

"Sebastian?"

He wrenched his attention back to her face. "Yes?"

"I said, if you've come to drag me back to work, I'm not going without a fight."

For a second, the notion of tossing her over his shoulder and carrying her back to his suite blocked every sane thought in his head. "I'm not paying you to sit by the pool."

"Then consider this a vacation day. I have plenty to burn."

"You picked a hell of a time to go AWOL."

She sighed. "Everything is organized. The summit doesn't start until the cocktail party tonight. There's plenty of time for me to have a little fun. You should, too."

"I'm not here to have fun," he reminded her.

She wrinkled her nose. "Yes, I know. But you're so pre-pared you could probably do the entire summit in your sleep. Why don't you relax a little today?"

"How do you suggest I do that?"

She stopped in the act of spreading lotion on her arm and brought her gaze to bear on him. The unbridled hope in her eyes twisted his gut. Was he that much of a tyrant?

"You could start by buying me a drink."

"It's ten o'clock in the morning."

She snapped the lid of the suntan lotion closed and picked up a beige sun hat, adorned with blue forget-me-nots. Once she set it on her head, the wide brim hid her expression from him.

"Make it an orange juice."

Sebastian held his hand out to Missy and braced himself for the contact with her skin. She wiped lotion from her palms before giving Sebastian her hand. As expected, a pulse of fire sped up his arm and struck below his belt. He released her before the temptation to pull her close gave him away. Instead, he set his palm at the small of her back and nudged her toward the tiki-style bar.

From beneath her ruddy lashes, she peered his way. "I'm sorry I ran off without telling you this morning."

"I'm sorry you felt you had to."

"Am I hearing things or did the never-wrong Sebastian Case just apologize to his lowly assistant?" Laughter bright-ened the green in her eyes.

"I'm wrong on occasion and am not such an ass that I can't admit it." Driven by compulsions too strong to fight, he grazed his fingertips upward until he encountered bare skin. "And you are far from lowly."

A faint tremor beneath his hand told him she found the skin-to-skin contact as disturbing as he did. This attraction between them was a distraction he couldn't afford.

He directed her on top of the only empty stool and stood

behind her. Her sun-warmed shoulder brushed his chest as he leaned forward to order her a drink, increasing his temperature even further. With a dismayed sound, she scooted away.

"You're going to ruin your suit if you get suntan lotion on it."

"I don't care."

"How can you not care?" she countered. "You spend a fortune on your clothes."

He lifted a shoulder. He'd ruin a hundred suits if it meant being close to her. The scent of suntan lotion rising off her skin aroused the craving to strip that boring bathing suit off her body and determine if the sun had marked her gorgeous pale flesh.

She gasped as he hooked a finger beneath her bathing suit strap and tugged it out of place. "What are you doing?"

"Making sure you aren't getting too much sun."

"When you touch me, I have trouble thinking straight," she whispered.

Her admission awakened a rumble of pleasure. "You shouldn't say things like that."

"I don't understand what's going on between us."

Nor did he. "Nothing is going on."

"We made love last night."

It took a great deal of effort, but he locked away his erotic musings. "It should never have happened."

"But it did." She met his gaze, her eyes soft with curiosity.

She wanted to know why he'd made love to her when he'd been so determined it was the wrong thing to do. He hadn't quite answered that question for himself. He could blame it on intense sexual chemistry, but that wouldn't be the whole truth. Grasping the whole truth might just lead him into uncharted territory where his assistant was concerned.

A familiar figure emerged from the pool and reminded Sebastian that he had more problems at hand than his wayward assistant. "Did my mother give you any hint of what my father is really doing here?"

Reeling from what she'd glimpsed in Sebastian's somber gray eyes, Missy scrambled to reorient her thoughts. "She said your dad went golfing this morning. I assumed they came here on vacation."

"He took Lucas Smythe golfing. Probably intends to talk him out of selling Smythe Industries to us."

Missy's chest tightened. Sebastian's relationship with his father was uneasy. During the years she worked for the eldest Case son, she'd had a front-row seat to Sebastian's battle with his father over business strategies and the direction the company should move in the future.

When Brandon's health problems had surfaced and he'd announced his plans to retire, Missy had assumed Sebastian and Max would at last have the chance to run things their way. Then the surprise announcement—Brandon had convinced Nathan to return to Houston and join the family business.

Although everyone at the company knew Nathan was a half brother to Max and Sebastian, Missy suspected she was the only one outside the family who knew that Nathan was a love child produced by Brandon's long-time mistress who died when Nathan was twelve.

Because Missy had gotten to know Sebastian's mother fairly well, Susan had discussed those early days when her husband first insisted that Nathan move in with them. Missy wasn't sure she could have put aside her hurt and anger at a husband's betrayal the way Susan had. In fact, she'd treated Nathan no differently than if he'd been her own son.

Nor had her biological sons made things any easier. Susan had described a house in turmoil. Sebastian and Max were old enough to understand how deeply their father had hurt their mother and resented the appearance of a half brother that didn't belong. Bitterness led to bad behavior. It was no surprise when Nathan took off after college. And from what Missy had gathered, he might have stayed away if Brandon's heart problems hadn't grown serious. Too bad having Nathan work for Case Consolidated Holdings was just the first of many times Brandon had interfered since his retirement.

"My father's planning on attending the summit," Sebastian continued.

"Are you going to be okay?" She put her hand on his arm, sympathy spilling into her voice.

"Fine." His terse reply was typical of how Sebastian coped with any emotion having to do with his father. Shut it down and pretend nothing's wrong.

She offered up an inaudible sigh to St. Monica, the patron saint her mother often prayed to for patience. "This is your summit, Sebastian. He won't interfere."

"He's here, isn't he?" His gaze shifted from her to his mother. "He's already interfering."

"Maybe he won't."

"Stop being so damned positive."

Rarely, in all the years that they'd worked together had she dared physical contact. Sebastian wasn't the sort of person who invited anyone to enter his space.

But last night, a shift had happened. A connection, however tenuous, had formed between them. Before she considered her actions, she dropped her hand from his arm to his thigh. His focus swung toward her. A quick squeeze and she had his complete attention.

"Missy." Her name sighed out of him, a weary, reluctant sound that spoke of weakening resistance.

Delight found its way around her guards and set up camp inside her heart. If she was smart, she'd shut it down. No good would come of flirting with Sebastian. This thing between them had nowhere to go. She should be content with their one night together. But her willpower was a fickle thing where he was concerned.

"Yes, Sebastian?"

"I can't focus with your hand on my thigh."

"Seems to me you're focusing just fine." The long muscle beneath her fingers tensed.

He trapped her hand beneath his. His touch heated her as hot as the Nevada desert in July and baked her mouth dry. The crowd gathered around the pool vanished as she lost herself in the pull of his charismatic allure.

"What I mean is I can't focus on the problems at hand."

"I thought I was your problem at hand." She tried a smile.

His shoulders relaxed. "Only one of them."

"Stop worrying so much," she coaxed. "Enjoy the moment."

"That's not the way I work and you know it."

"Maybe you should try something different and see how it goes."

"I'd love for it to be that easy, but it's not." He carried her hand back to her side and patted it. "I'm not going to take advantage of the situation."

No, he was too damned honorable to take advantage no matter how much she pleaded for him to do so. Why had she picked such an upright guy to get worked up about? Because his principles contributed to his appeal. She'd be proud to bring Sebastian home to meet her father. He would see the same admirable qualities she did and approve.

Too bad Sebastian was out of her league.

"Your mother spotted us," she said, waving back at Susan.

Sebastian nodded. "Grab your drink. Let's go."

The air cooled dramatically without Sebastian's warmth beside her. She trailed after him, her untouched orange juice clutched in her hand.

"Hello, darling." Dressed in a black one-piece that showed off her athletic figure, Susan Case offered her cheek for Sebastian's kiss. "Never expected to see you by the pool. Of course, you're not really dressed for it, now, are you?"

"Not exactly."

The easy affection between mother and son made Missy smile. Sebastian treated his mother with relentless charm. He was at his most unguarded around Susan. The first time Missy had ever seen them together had been the moment her hopeless crush on Sebastian had begun. Her brothers had been that way with their mother, reverent and affectionate. The same behavior spilled over into how they treated their wives.

She knew Sebastian would treat his wife with similar adoration if he ever married again. The thought hammered her confidence flat. No use wishing she could be the woman who captured Sebastian's heart. He would probably choose someone like his mother. Sophisticated, elegant, gracious, and well connected. A nobody like her wouldn't have a chance in hell of surviving in his circles.

"Sebastian, it was good of you to let Missy have some time off for a little fun. You work her too hard."

"I didn't give her time off," Sebastian growled. "She took it."

Susan's brows rose. "Well, then good for her. You should follow her example. I'm getting tense just looking at you."

No one but his mother could speak to Sebastian like that and get away with it. Missy bit the inside of her cheeks to contain a grin.

"Then perhaps I should return to work and leave you two to enjoy the sunshine."

"You're letting me stay?" Missy asked.

He shot his mother a severe look. "It seems I don't have much choice."

Susan watched the exchange with interest. When her son was out of earshot, she turned to Missy. "I thought he'd never go. Let's order some cocktails. Then perhaps you'll tell me what's going on between you two."

Sebastian had just finished up a conference call with Max and their financially troubled overseas supplier when his

mother sauntered into the suite. She'd come straight from
the pool and smelled of sunshine and chlorine. She loved the
water and kept in shape by swimming two miles each day.

"Can you break long enough to take your mother to lunch?"

Sebastian checked behind her, half expecting to see Missy
using his mother as a protective shield. "Just you?"

Sebastian cursed as speculation lit up his mother's eyes.
Sometimes her romantic nature went on overdrive. That was
fine for Nathan, who was happily married. Or Max, who'd
vowed loudly and often that he had no intention of ever tying
the knot. But Sebastian had no issues with finding the right
woman and settling down to raise a few kids. He just didn't
want his mother pushing available females at him while he
searched.

"Just me." His mother offered him an off-center grin. "I
had a few things I wanted to discuss with you."

Sebastian raised his eyebrows. "Such as?"

"Missy told me what happened last night."

Annoyance tightened his gut into stone, but Sebastian decided to play dumb and see just how much she'd told his
mother. "She told you she quit?"

"She told me she had too much to drink while celebrating
her birthday and threw herself at you but that you were too
professional to take advantage of her." Susan's eyes narrowed.
"That's a lot of bull, isn't it?"

"I'm not going to discuss it."

"Is that why she's quitting?"

"No."

"Sebastian, I don't know what to say." And yet she continued talking. "This isn't like you."

On that they both agreed. "I'm still not discussing this with
you."

His mother kept going as if he'd never spoken. "She has a
boyfriend. Did you think for one minute how much trouble
this will create between them?"

"They broke up."

"So, she was on the rebound." His mother tried for stern, but something sparkled in her eyes. "Oh, Sebastian. How could you take advantage of her in such a vulnerable state?"

He could clear his name by revealing that Missy had been the one to proposition him, but he refused to defend himself at the risk of her reputation.

Before he could answer, his mother changed her line of questioning. "What are you going to do about Kaitlyn?"

There was nothing to do about Kaitlyn. His mother had it in her head that he was involved with her. That couldn't be further from the truth. They were casually involved, emphasis on casual.

Sure, marriage to Kaitlyn made sense in a lot of ways. They attended the same charity galas and came from similar backgrounds. She would fit seamlessly into his life. But most important, he needed someone that soothed his spirit, not aggravated it. And Kaitlyn possessed a tranquil quality, rare among women. She'd make an ideal wife.

That made him question why, when he pictured a woman living in his home and sharing his bed, he imagined her with red hair.

"Kaitlyn and I are friends, Mother. Nothing more." Tired of being on the defensive, Sebastian changed topics. "Why are you and Dad here?"

His mother held his gaze for a long moment before answering. "He regrets retiring and wants to return to work."

Annoyance kicked Sebastian in the temple. A sharp pulse began in his head. "As CEO?"

"He said no. He claims he wants to return part time so he has something to occupy him besides golf."

And once he came back to the company, Brandon would undermine Sebastian at every turn until he got fed up and stepped down. Bile rose in his throat. He should have known his father would pull something like this.

"You need to talk him out of it." His mother put her hand on his arm. Her blue eyes widened with concern. "I almost lost him a year ago. He promised me we'd travel and make up for all the years he wasn't around."

Brandon's twelve-year affair with Nathan's mother had taken a severe toll on his wife. Sebastian had often wondered what bargain his parents had made that had kept them together and had convinced his mother to raise her husband's illegitimate son.

"As much as it benefits both of us for Dad to stay far away from Case Consolidated Holdings," Sebastian said, "I'm not sure how I'm supposed to stop him from returning to work."

"Talk to him. Make him understand that you're doing a wonderful job running the company."

His mother's optimism made Sebastian shake his head. Her husband rarely thought about anyone's needs besides his own unless forced to do so.

"He showed up for the leadership summit, and I'm sure he intends for it to appear as if he's still in charge. He took Lucas Smythe golfing and probably spent the entire round badmouthing my leadership abilities. You don't seriously believe anything I say will sway him, do you?"

Sebastian refused to battle his father this week in front of all the executives.

"Do what you can."

With those words, his mother left to shower and change for their lunch. Sebastian was staring at the Vegas strip when Missy emerged from her room.

Her expression shifted from cheerful to uncertain when she spotted his frown. "What's wrong?"

"Did you have a fun morning with my mother?"

"As a matter of fact I did." Missy crossed to the table he'd been working at all morning. "Are you mad because I had fun or because it was with your mother?"

She set her cell phone down and used her finger to spin it

Today's outfit of jeans and a snug white T-shirt had about the same effect on his libido as the sexy black dress she'd worn last night. Russet waves, still damp from her shower, rested on her shoulders, turning the cotton fabric transparent.

Sebastian spied the straps from her simple white bra. It frustrated him that everything about her turned him on. How was he supposed to maintain a professional relationship with her when all he could think about was lifting her onto the conference table and checking her for tan lines?

"She's been lecturing me on taking advantage of you," he muttered, stepping near enough to touch her. Keeping his hands to himself tested his control, but he triumphed. "I thought I told you to leave it alone."

"You told me not to say anything to your father or Lucas Smythe."

He barely heard her. She'd interpreted his words literally to defy him. His annoyance with her behavior had yet to run its course.

"Only you didn't set things straight. You spun a story. An outrageous story."

"Not so outrageous," she said, her full lips drawn tight. With her impudent chin cocked at a belligerent angle, she concluded, "I'd just broken up with my boyfriend. It's not so hard to believe I got tipsy celebrating my birthday and hit on you, but you were the perfect gentleman and turned me down."

"And if I turned you down, how exactly did you explain why you were in my suite wearing my shirt?"

"Because I was naked when I climbed into bed with you."

Vivid images of exactly that leapt into his thoughts. Even without his eyes closed the evocative memories tormented him.

"I told you not to interfere." He gripped the back of a chair to keep from throttling her.

"If I hadn't, Lucas Smythe wouldn't know that you'd never take advantage of any employee, drunk or sober." For good measure, she added, "Your mother promised to help me straighten out the misunderstanding."

"There was no misunderstanding." Sebastian knew Lucas Smythe would never believe such a ridiculous story. Who in their right mind could resist a naked Missy? "But now it looks like I'm making excuses for my behavior."

His sharp tone eviscerated her composure. She set her hands on her hips. Her brow puckered. "Can't you trust me to handle this?"

"No."

"This is just typical of you."

She'd never had the nerve to criticize him before. Apparently an abundance of sexy curves wasn't the only thing his assistant had been keeping from him.

"What do you mean?"

"If you're not the one in control of a situation, you don't think it's being handled correctly."

Her accusation fell on deaf ears. If she'd hoped to stir his temper, she'd taken the wrong tack. He'd heard it all before. Being the one in control had led Case Consolidated Holdings to higher profitability and kept his personal life calm and peaceful. He wasn't going to surrender the power without a down and dirty fight.

"That's what makes me successful."

"In business maybe."

He smirked at her. "What else is there?"

"There's your personal life," she retorted, her color high. "Maybe if you didn't have to be in charge all the time, something wonderful might happen."

"Are you referring to last night when I let you set the terms for that ridiculous bet?"

Head held high, she blew out air with a disparaging noise, but her hunched shoulders told a different story. "I'll bet the only reason you agreed to the wager in the first place is because you thought I'd lose."

"Haven't you learned that bets between us don't work out?"

"Maybe not for you," she said, her voice losing much of its vigor. "But I don't regret what happened between us."

"I can't say the same."

"So, if you had to do it all over again?" She spoke slowly as if the weight of the words made the question hard to ask.

"I'd have left you home." Why deny it? If she hadn't come, he never would have been sucked into her rebellion. Never would have made love to her. And he certainly wouldn't feel like a poker player down to his last dollar.

"I'm sorry you feel that way," she said, her brisk tone almost masking the throb in her voice. "For what it's worth, I'm glad I came. I'm glad we spent the night together. It made me realize that Tim was right. I have been preoccupied with you ever since we started working together. Without these past two days I would be questioning my decision to quit. Now, I'm confident I made the right decision."

"You didn't. We're a good team." Sebastian barely recognized himself reflected in her eyes. She was right about him needing to control everything. He liked his life neat and without distractions. Until yesterday, she'd understood. "I'm not giving up on persuading you to stay."

She looked surprised. "We've done nothing but fight."

"We're not fighting. We're on opposite sides of an issue we both feel strongly about."

"How is that not fighting?"

He lowered his voice. "I don't want to fight with you." No indeed. He wanted her in his arms, surrendering to his kisses. The realization infuriated him. He shoved his hands in his pockets to stop himself from reaching for her.

Her body lost its stiffness. "I don't want to fight with you, either."

"How can we come to an understanding?"

"You could let me get on with my career and give me a glowing recommendation."

"Or?" he prompted.

"There is no or." Her lips formed the saddest smile he'd ever seen. "I think we both know there's no going back from what happened."

While Sebastian grappled for words to change her mind, Missy exited the suite, successfully ending the conversation with the last word.

The cell phone she'd left on the table buzzed. Sebastian pulled the phone toward him and checked the display. Instead of it being someone from the office or a member of the hotel staff about the arrangements, the incoming number belonged to someone named Tim. The boyfriend. Wasn't he out of the picture?

The call went to voice mail. Sebastian didn't hesitate before hitting speed dial to listen to the message.

"Hey, babe."

Babe?

Sebastian couldn't picture anyone calling Missy by that pet name.

"I just realized I missed your birthday. I know you must be pretty pissed at me, but I want you to know that I still care about you."

That wasn't the speech of a man who was done with his ex-girlfriend but one who was covering his bases in case things didn't work out with the new squeeze. Sebastian deleted the message. An ex-boyfriend unable to make a clean break was only going to distract her. He needed her focused on the leadership summit this week—and on him.

Five

At seven, Sebastian surveyed the transformed suite. Two fully stocked bars awaited guests. Wait staff flanked tables loaded with mouthwatering finger food. The atmosphere was relaxed and elegant.

Missy had come through again. He'd never really doubted that she would.

Even if the scent of her perfume hadn't reached his nose, the way his nerves began to buzz told him she was close by. Sweetness and sin. An intoxicating blend that made him crazy.

"Everything is exactly as we discussed," she said from behind him, her crisp tones reassuring Sebastian that his efficient assistant had returned to the fold.

"Good."

He glanced over his shoulder and saw a goddess. Missy wore a strapless dress with alternating bands of black and white sequins that hugged all her curves and emphasized the fiery brilliance of her hair. She'd pinned it up. The sleek updo emphasized her long, elegant neck and the delicate hollows below her collarbones.

Cool and composed, she regarded him through eyes more brown than hazel tonight. Hard to believe this tranquil beauty was the same spitfire that propositioned him last night. His senses crowed in appreciation of every luscious inch of her while his thoughts grumbled about unnecessary distractions.

Where had his practical assistant gone? The old Missy had taken his orders without question. She'd never distracted him from working with her intoxicating perfume or her provocative curves.

"Is this what you're planning on wearing tonight?" Frustration with her allure jolted the blunt question out of him.

"Yes." Her curt reply told him she had not appreciated his tone. "Why?"

"It's not exactly appropriate for a business meeting."

Picking a fight with her was simple self-preservation. He needed her as annoyed with him as he was attracted to her. Otherwise, the door that separated his suite from her hotel room wouldn't be much of an obstacle for him later.

"This is a cocktail party." She inclined her head, her tone vibrating with restraint.

"And you're my employee, not my date."

Her eyes widened at his severe tone. "I'm aware of that."

"Are you?"

"Of course." She looked piqued that he'd even ask. "You don't think I got the message loud and clear earlier?"

"What message?"

"That I'm not your type and this attraction between us has nowhere to go."

"What makes you say that?"

She rolled her eyes. "Come on, look at the women you date when you take the time for a social life. They're all sophisticated, beautiful, wealthy, and half-starved to fit into all those gorgeous designer clothes."

Yet not one of them stirred his blood the way Missy did.

"It's okay," she continued. "I'm not in your league. I never thought I was." When he didn't deny her claim, the corners of her lips wobbled before achieving a brave smile. "I never expected anything beyond last night."

And that's exactly how it should be. So, why did his mood sour at her admission?

"Forgive me if I find that difficult to believe when you were wandering around here in my shirt and nothing else this morning. Were you hoping I'd spend the day in bed with you? Our deal was for one night."

Her eyes widened in dismay, but her clenched fists told Sebastian she wasn't going to be cowed by his bad mood. "And one night is all you're going to get."

"All *I'm* going to get?" He leaned forward, feeling her sharp inhalation like a punch to his solar plexus. Her parted lips drove him mad with longing. He wanted to taste her again. Cherries and lemons. The memory of her kisses was carved into his brain. "The bet and the terms were your decision, not mine."

"You went along with it happily enough," she shot back.

Why were they fighting when all he wanted was to haul her tight against him and claim her mouth? "I didn't think I was going to lose."

"But you did."

"And I honored my part of the bargain."

Her eyes almost popped out of her head. Her mouth opened and closed like a fish on land. Her hands formed tight fists at her sides.

"Well, excuse me for forcing you to have sex with me."

Seeing that she was completely exasperated with him, Sebastian pulled her phone out of his pocket and extended it. "You left this behind earlier." She took the phone, but he didn't let go. Fighting with her hadn't eased his suffering. In fact, he wanted her more than ever. The urge to sweep her into his bedroom and find out what she was wearing under that black and white dress was close to driving him mad. "Someone named Tim called you."

"Tim called?" Obviously that gave her hope that their relationship wasn't over. Her lashes lowered to her cheeks but not fast enough for Sebastian to miss the delight shining in her eyes.

Annoyance growled like a cornered badger. "I suppose he wants you back."

She reined in her emotions until nothing showed in her expression. "I doubt that. He broke up with me because he found his soul mate online." She checked her phone's display. "There's no voice mail. I'll bet he called because he wants his anime collection back."

"Maybe he forgot to wish you a belated birthday."

"Maybe." Missy's gaze sliced to Sebastian. "Did you listen to my messages? You did." She speed dialed and put the phone to her ear. "And deleted one from Tim."

He stared at her impassively.

She shook the cell phone at him. "Why?"

"You deserve better."

"Did it ever occur to you that I can't do better?"

Is that what she thought? From her downturned lips, Sebastian gathered that's exactly what she believed. Foolish girl. She was better than a hundred Tims put together.

"Any man would be proud to call you his girlfriend."

"Any man but you." The slight lilt at the end of her statement made it sound more as if she asked a question.

Sebastian ignored the desire to assure her that he had not excluded himself. To tell her that would create possibilities, and he couldn't do that to her. He needed an executive assistant—not a lover or a girlfriend.

"I'd like you to change," he said.

"And I'd like world peace. Seems neither one of us is going to get what they want tonight." A smile curved her lips, but her eyes resembled granite. "Excuse me. I'd better make sure everything's perfect."

Once again her cheeky attitude left him without a comeback. She slipped past him and headed toward the buffet table. He stared after her, the delectable sway of her hips turning his mouth into a sand trap. He remembered trailing his fingertips from her nape to the small of her back. She'd shivered. Her body's reactions had been exquisite, delicate perfection.

With an impatient snort, Sebastian headed for the bar and ordered a scotch.

An hour later, he stood on the opposite side of the suite's living room from Missy and made small talk with the president of their hydro division and his wife. His assistant hadn't glanced his way once since walking away from their conversation. She'd drifted through the crowd, exchanging pleasantries with everyone, laughing and charming each guest and acting as if Sebastian was no more to her than a piece of furniture.

Her snub battered his pride. He regretted inferring that he'd felt obligated to sleep with her last night, but she had to believe that nothing like that was going to happen again.

A cleared throat brought Sebastian back to his companions. He swiveled his head and found two pairs of curious eyes on him. "I'm sorry. Did you say something?"

Owen Darby shot his wife a wry look. "I was just saying that I didn't recognize Missy when I first saw her. She looks wonderful."

"She did something different with her hair," Sebastian said.

"And she got rid of her glasses," Owen added.

"Her dress is fabulous," Alicia Darby said. "She has terrific taste."

Sebastian's attention slid toward the source of his frustration. "Yes, I suppose she does."

"I hear you're going to be an uncle," Alicia said. "Your mother is excited about the new addition to your family."

Nathan's wife, Emma, was pregnant. Sebastian smiled to cover his wince. His future niece or nephew wasn't related to his mother by blood, but that didn't stop her from being thrilled. Susan Case had been looking forward to grandchildren for a long time. She'd hidden her upset, but Sebastian had seen the shadow in his mom's eyes each time Chandra had enacted her pregnancy dramas when he brought up the topic of divorce.

After two years, he'd ended his marriage almost as much for his mother's sanity as for his own. He couldn't put her through any more disappointment. She longed to be a grandmother. That's why she was so excited about Nathan's child. She would love it the way she'd loved Nathan when he came to live with them.

Sebastian pushed aside old bitterness. Resenting his mother for being a loving, generous person was wrong on so many levels. "She's already setting up a nursery so she can babysit."

Alicia gave a wistful sigh. "Do they know if it's a boy or a girl?"

"Not yet." Talking about the baby was no more comfortable for Sebastian than discussing Missy's makeover. Every time his mother mentioned the things she was planning once the baby came, he calculated how old his own son or daughter would have been if Chandra had actually been pregnant when he married her as she'd claimed. Or if she'd gotten pregnant at any time during their two-year marriage. "I think my mother's hoping for a girl. She complains all the time about how she missed out on the fun girly things by having all boys."

"I know all about that," Alicia said. "I have two boys of my own who love to hunt, fish, golf and do all the same things their father enjoys." She smiled up at her husband to take the sting out of her words. "But they are my pride and joy. I just wish they'd get married and start giving me some granddaughters."

Sebastian's attention wandered in Missy's direction once

more. She'd cornered Lucas Smythe. From the expression on the old man's face, Sebastian guessed Missy was feeding him the same improbable tale she'd told his mother. Why couldn't she just do as he'd asked and leave the matter alone?

He excused himself from the Darbys, but was intercepted by the president of the chemical division. By the time he extricated himself from that conversation, Missy had disappeared. Nor did she return to the party. As the wait staff cleaned up and then left, he half hoped that with the guests gone she'd reappear and they could continue…

What? Fighting? Making love?

Sebastian tugged his tie askew with a growl.

Wearing her favorite pair of pajamas, with her hair scraped back into a ponytail and her black framed glasses perched on her nose, Missy stared at the door connecting to Sebastian's suite and wondered if she could ignore her boss's summons.

"Missy, open the door. I need to speak to you."

With Sebastian, it was always about him. What about what she needed?

She kicked her legs free of the covers and stalked across the room. "What about?" She called through the door. He'd been a jerk all evening and she wasn't exactly dressed to receive visitors.

"You left the party early. Are you all right?"

The steel in her spine bowed a little. "I'm fine. Just tired." She rested her cheek against the door. "I didn't get a lot of sleep last night."

She didn't mean to make the remark flirtatious, yet a cascade of sparks trickled along her nerves.

"Please open the door." Less demanding, more like a request.

"I'm not sure that's a good idea."

"Why not?"

"Because I'm in my pajamas."

The silence on the other side of the door lasted so long Missy wondered if he'd left. Disappointment stormed her defenses. How was she supposed to act as if the night before meant nothing to her when she hung on his every word and look?

"Show me."

At first she thought she'd misheard him. "What?"

"Show me."

What was his game? "You don't believe I'm dressed for bed?"

"I believe you. I'm just curious what you wear."

She was hot and bothered before he uttered his last syllable. Damn him. She hadn't done any flirting since high school. Her relationship with Tim had been straightforward and uneventful. He'd never given her heart palpitations or made her wet with a single glance.

Missy unbolted and threw open the door. "Here I am."

Sebastian slouched, his shoulder against the wall. With his tie pulled off center and his dark hair falling forward to obscure his eyes, he looked as tired as she felt. Her caretaker gene kicked in. He had a full week ahead of him and should be in bed instead of standing outside her door. But she quashed the urge to tell him to go get some sleep. She was not his girlfriend or his mother.

"Somehow I knew you'd be wearing red." His weary tone was at odds with the simmer in his gray eyes as he trailed his gaze from her chin to her toes. "Are those palm trees?"

"And surf boards. My brother brought them back from Hawaii."

Despite the conservative nature of her sleepwear, Missy felt edgy and vulnerable. She had no doubts that if he touched her she was a goner. But why would he? Sebastian had emphasized that he was done with her. So, why was he standing at her door so late?

"Is there something else?" she prompted, eager for him to

leave. Her muscles shivered with restrained impulses. The longer he stayed, the harder to resist the urge to grab his tie and haul him to her bed. "Because I'm really, really tired."

Earlier, he'd been right when he'd accused her of wanting to spend the day with him. Four years of suppressed longing hadn't been assuaged by a mere ten hours of lovemaking. In fact, the night with Sebastian had fueled her appetite for more.

"Missy—"

She cut him off. "Don't you dare." Something about the way he said her name spurred her to action. The urge to hit him came out of nowhere. Her fist connected with his chest.

"What the hell was that for?" His eyes flared to life, but he looked more surprised than angry.

"I don't know."

She'd sensed whatever he'd been about to say would persuade her to get naked. That couldn't happen. One night with him was about fulfilling dozens upon dozens of erotic fantasies. A week would mean she'd fallen prey to the same unrealistic pipe dream that had gotten her heart broken in high school.

She didn't fit into Sebastian's world any more than she'd fit into Chip's. Repeating the pattern would be idiotic. She liked to think she'd gotten wiser since age sixteen. This morning with Sebastian, she'd discovered how close she'd come to making the same mistake all over again.

He fingered the spot where she'd struck him. "I was going to compliment you on how well the cocktail party went. I couldn't have pulled this week off without you."

Confusion reigned. Is that really what he'd intended to say? If so, she'd just made a fool of herself again. If not...

No. She couldn't think about the alternative. Sebastian had made his need for her clear. She was his assistant. That's the only role he wanted her to play.

"Thank you."

"What will it take for you to stay on? More money? A company car? An extra week of vacation? I'll give you anything you want."

She wanted him to make her feel like a desirable woman, not a valuable commodity because she was organized and detail oriented.

"Anything?" It intrigued her to see the uncompromising Sebastian offer her a blank check.

"Anything." His low voice slid over her skin like warm silk. She recalled its effect on her the night before. He'd coaxed her to do things that even now roused goose bumps.

She kept her tone level so he wouldn't see how he disturbed her. "Good thing Nathan's in charge of acquisitions because you suck at negotiating."

"Not usually, but something about you brings out the worst in me."

"I never used to," she complained softly.

"You also never used to come to work dressed like you were tonight, either." Hard as iron, his eyes held hers. "What is it going to take to keep you on as my assistant?"

She pondered the long hours at her desk and the price she'd paid in her personal life. She'd made the decision to quit before she'd slept with Sebastian. Nothing had changed. In fact, moving on was more essential than ever.

"It's no use. You might promise me the same thing won't happen again, but I know it will. You just can't help yourself."

His eyebrows arched. "You think I can't keep my hands off you?"

At his misunderstanding, her body flushed asphalt-in-August hot. "I'm not talking about sex, I'm talking about your promise not to bother me evenings and weekends. You'd start regressing. I want to work for someone who understands that an employee's off-hours are sacred." She tossed her head. "In fact, someone already made me an offer. Someone who knows the value of a personal life."

"Who?"

"Nothing's finalized yet. But when it is, you'll be the first to know."

Donning a plum-colored dress, Missy slipped out of her hotel room at six-thirty to make sure she missed Sebastian. After yesterday, she needed a cup or two of coffee before she faced him.

Missy reached the ballroom where most of the summit meetings would take place. After checking on the food arrangements and making sure all the audiovisual equipment was working, she assured herself that Sebastian's opening speech awaited him at the podium. Everything had to be perfect.

"I see my son has you burning the candle at both ends." Brandon stood at the back of the room, dressed for a round of golf rather than a business meeting. "Have you given any more thought to my suggestion that you take over for Dean as director of communications? Max liked the idea and wants to discuss it with you after the summit."

"I'm not sure I have the experience required," Missy hedged, wondering if she should even be discussing a job change without talking to Sebastian first. The opportunity tempted her, but she'd be happier about it if the idea had come from Sebastian.

Working for a family business, regardless of size, offered challenges. As Sebastian's executive assistant, Missy had often found herself trapped in the middle of a power play between her boss and the head of the company. Since Brandon had stepped down as CEO, her job had grown less complicated politically, but he still owned a large share of the company and of late had begun to insinuate himself back into the business with frequent visits to the office and happily offered opinions.

He'd escalated his interference by taking Lucas Smythe

golfing yesterday. Not that Missy believed he'd come right out and tell Smythe not to sell his company to Case Consolidated Holdings. But involving himself by talking with Max about the communications director position was a pretty overt act. Was Sebastian right? Did his father want to be in charge once more?

Brandon dismissed her concerns with a wave. "Don't sell yourself short. I've watched you these past four years. Your talents are wasted on my son."

"I'm not sure Sebastian would agree." But the truth was she had no idea if her boss appreciated her or just took her for granted.

"You let Max and me worry about Sebastian." Brandon held the door so she could exit the ballroom. "You'd make an outstanding director of communications."

Missy was flattered that someone had recognized her skills. She'd graduated two years ago with a degree in business and a minor in journalism. Her background made the position a dream job.

Too bad Sebastian liked her right where she was.

"I appreciate your faith in me," she said as they strolled down the hallway that led to the hotel's atrium and casino.

"You should have been promoted years ago. I know you'll do a great job."

And she would. Much better than the guy who'd held the position for the past three years. But staying at Case Consolidated Holdings meant seeing Sebastian all the time. How was she supposed to get over her feelings for him and move on in her personal life with daily reminders of how amazing they'd been together?

Missy lifted her hand to hide a yawn. Sleep had eluded her for a long time last night. Sebastian's visit had left her keyed up and wide awake. Damn the man for being so aggravating and attractive. Her seesawing emotions were a source of utter frustration.

"Are you playing golf again this morning?"

"No. I thought I'd stick around and listen to Sebastian give the opening speech."

Wincing in sympathy for her boss, Missy forced a bright smile. "It's a good one. You'll be impressed."

"I'm sure it's wonderful. Did you help him write it?"

"I offered a couple suggestions." In fact, she'd created the first draft and Sebastian had revised it to suit his style.

"I'm sure you did." Brandon put his arm around her shoulders and squeezed. "Have fun with the ladies today."

In addition to making sure the conference arrangements were hitch-free, she had the job of playing social director for the executives' wives. Today's schedule called for a sightseeing trip to the Hoover Dam. Then lunch followed by the Haunted Vegas tour.

Brandon winked. "Don't let them get you into too much trouble."

With that cryptic remark ringing in her ears, Missy watched Sebastian's father head toward the casino. She had almost an hour before she was to meet the wives for breakfast. Yesterday she'd won another two thousand dollars. The windfall was burning a hole in her purse. A little gambling would go a long way toward distracting her from what had just happened with Sebastian.

Lucky at cards, unlucky at love.

Missy had become a walking, talking example of that idiom. Fetching a twenty from her wallet, she cruised the slot machines, looking for a likely candidate. The first machine swallowed her money like a party girl guzzling imported champagne. Thirty minutes later, she was down five hundred. Sighing over her change of luck, Missy checked her watch. She had fifteen minutes before she was supposed to meet the wives. Time enough to feed one last crisp twenty into a slot machine.

At the center of the casino, a couple dozen machines

surrounded a bright-blue, convertible Ford Mustang. Picking one at random, Missy fed in her twenty. Four spins later, she had resigned herself to walking away when five gold coins lined up in a row and her machine began whooping like a pack of crazed football fans with their team poised to score the game-winning touchdown.

"You won a car." Gloria Smythe stood next to her, wearing a big smile.

Missy had met her last night at the cocktail party and liked her immediately. The vivacious blonde was twenty years younger than her imposing husband and smiled as much as he frowned.

"I did?"

"Sure looks that way to me."

And the way the bells were sounding and the lights pulsed with frantic enthusiasm, Missy was starting to agree. She'd just won a car. Why wasn't she jumping up and down in delirious excitement?

Because nothing compared to the thrill she'd felt in Sebastian's arms.

Missy shook herself out of her mooning. Pining over a man she couldn't have was idiotic. "What do I do now?"

"I think that nice young man coming this way will have you fill out some paperwork."

"I don't have time." Missy spotted a skinny guy with a shaved head in his twenties heading her way. "I'm supposed to meet everyone in ten minutes."

"Don't worry about that." Gloria smiled.

"But the tour is scheduled to leave no later than nine, and I'm supposed to be on the bus to make sure all of you have a great time."

"Don't you worry about that. Fill out the paperwork and come find us in the restaurant over there. We're sitting on the patio."

Missy stared at Gloria's back as she sauntered away. That wasn't where they were supposed to meet. What was going on?

Thirty minutes later, with her paperwork done, Missy wound between the tables of the most expensive of the three restaurants open for breakfast. Bordered on two sides by French doors that offered access to the outside dining, the rattan furnishings, potted palms and soothing green and white color scheme gave the space a comfortable, relaxed feel.

Missy spotted two tables of women on the patio just as Gloria had said. The day promised to be in the upper seventies, but at eight in the morning, the cooler temperature required sweaters and light jackets. Missy shivered in her sleeveless dress.

All conversation ceased as a couple of the women spotted her. Heads turned in her direction.

"We heard you won a car!" Susan Case said. "Congratulations."

"Thanks. Are you ready to go on the Hoover Dam tour?" Missy gazed at each of the women. A few wouldn't meet her eyes. Most grinned at her. Three frowned.

"We've decided to pass," said a woman with teased black hair and enormous sunglasses.

"In fact, we're not going to do any of the tours," Alicia Darby added. "But don't let us stop you from going."

Missy shook her head. "I don't understand. A lot of planning went into your itinerary."

"And we appreciate it," Gloria said. "But for most of us, our lives are busy and hectic."

Alicia nodded. "The last thing we want to do is go on vacation and have to do a bunch of sightseeing."

Missy imagined Sebastian's annoyance with this turn of events. He'd given her the task of making sure the wives were happy. "What do you want to do instead?"

"Go shopping."

"Spend a day at the spa."

"Lie around the pool."

"Drink."

"Gamble."

The answers came at her like bullets from a machine gun.

Missy didn't blame the women for wanting to relax and have fun. Isn't that what she'd ditched work to do yesterday? "Can I make arrangements for spa treatments or arrange transportation for shopping?"

Susan shook her head. "We're all set. Why don't you join us?"

The offer tempted her, but this morning she'd reminded herself that she wasn't on vacation. She really needed to stop acting like it. "I'm supposed to be working."

"You're supposed to be in charge of keeping us entertained," Gloria countered. "No reason you can't have a little fun at the same time."

True. Sebastian was already going to be unhappy when he found out they'd skipped the tours. So what did Missy have to lose?

She grinned. "Sure. That sounds like a lot of fun. But are you up for a little adventure?"

Several of the wives eyed her with interest.

Sebastian's mother, apparent spokeswoman for the group, spoke up. "We might be. What'd you have in mind?"

Six

When Sebastian returned to the suite at the end of that day's leadership summit, he poured himself a large scotch and stood at the window staring out at the Las Vegas strip. At five in the afternoon, the view lacked glitter.

His opening speech had gone well, despite the distraction of his father texting in the front row through the entire thing. But by the time Sebastian had finished speaking, he'd felt exactly like someone who'd barely snatched three hours of sleep two nights in a row.

During lunch he'd made the rounds and caught up to the executives he'd missed at the cocktail party the night before. Everyone commented on how well the summit was organized. Setting the schedule had been Missy's doing. Had he given her the credit she deserved?

Or had he simply taken for granted her superior organizational skills, her ability to anticipate his needs, her nonstop encouragement? She managed his calendar, kept track of mundane details and acted as his first line of defense so he could focus on the big picture. He'd given her access to every aspect of the business and control over some major aspects of his private life, like the decisions on the home he'd built. In doing so, he'd demonstrated his faith in her. But he wasn't sure he'd ever voiced his appreciation.

No wonder she'd quit.

"Sebastian?"

Missy's soft voice crossed twenty feet of hotel suite and tugged him back to the present. He glanced in her direction.

She'd poked her head through a narrow opening in the door that connected their rooms. A white towel was wrapped turban-like around her head. Did that mean she was fresh from a shower and that on the other side of the door she wore little more than a towel? Last time she'd appeared dressed like that, his lust for her had been fully sated. After thirty-six hours of celibacy, he wasn't convinced she'd be safe from him this time.

Grim and not the least amused by how fast his body tightened in reaction to his speculation, he swallowed the last of the scotch. It seared a path down his throat and straight into his belly.

"Were you expecting someone else?"

Her eyes widened. "I was hoping for nice-twin Sebastian instead of evil-twin Sebastian. Give me a ring when he shows up, won't you?"

To his surprise and amusement, she shut the door and he heard the decisive click of the lock as it engaged. "Damn her," he muttered, unable to fight a grin. In a matter of seconds she'd transformed his dark mood into something so much better. How did she do that with such minute effort?

He rapped on the closed door. As he waited for her to answer, he considered whether he would kiss her first or rip the towel from her body and then kiss her.

"Who is it?" she called.

"The big bad wolf," he called back.

"The three little pigs aren't in at the moment. Can I take a message?"

"Tell them I'm going to huff and puff and blow their house down unless you open this door."

"No can do. I'm afraid you'll eat me up."

"If you had any idea how true that was, you'd stay locked in there forever," he muttered, resting his forehead on the wood panel separating them.

The long silence that followed left Sebastian wondering if she'd heard him. Heart thumping, he waited, his muscles bunched in anticipation. When he heard the lock turn, he pushed back and waited for her to open the door.

To his intense disappointment, she wore a sophisticated cocktail dress of dark gold that bared her arms, showcased her tiny waist, and emphasized the flare of her hips. The color enticed gold highlights from the cinnamon locks tossed about her creamy shoulders.

"You look beautiful."

"I'm having a hard time reading you," she said. "One second you're my grumpy boss with high moral fiber, the next you're flirting with me. What's going on?"

He tugged her through the doorway and backed her up against the wall.

"You're driving me crazy, that's what."

"I'm driving you crazy?" She gazed up at him, eyes widened by his forceful handling. "How exactly?"

Gentling his touch, he coasted his palm up the generous slope of her hip to the valley of her waist, his caress aided by the silky material she wore. For all its sensual decadence, it couldn't compare to the hot, luxurious texture of her skin.

"You've changed since arriving in Las Vegas, both in looks and attitude," he said.

"And that's a bad thing?"

"It is when you wager five thousand dollars and a night with me on the turn of a roulette wheel."

"You could have said no."

"I'm not the sort who backs down from a challenge." He

grazed her collarbone with his fingers. "But you know that, don't you? In fact, you'd probably counted on it."

"Are you accusing me of something?"

He followed her neckline to the start of her cleavage. There, he picked up the gold locket he'd seen her wear many times. The piece of jewelry had never fascinated him when it had rested against fabric. Against her skin…that was another thing entirely.

"You played me."

"Hardly."

"You knew the instant I walked into the bar that I wanted you and you took advantage."

"Wait. Are you trying to tell me that I took advantage of you?" Her husky laugh made him mad with wanting. "Is that even possible?"

"It's possible."

Comprehension dawned in her eyes. "You want me."

He reached between them and cupped her breast, kneading the round contours. "I think we've established that." He eased his hips forward, letting her feel how much.

Her lashes fluttered and her breath hitched. He knew what would happen if he kissed her. They'd never make it to dinner, and he had two-dozen people converging on the restaurant at that very moment. This was his leadership summit. He was supposed to be playing host.

"And in your mind that's bad because what keeps your world all nice and tidy is me, working as your assistant." Her voice gained strength as she ferreted out all his secrets. "But you think I'm sexy."

"Missy."

She ignored his warning growl. "And you want to make love to me again."

"We have dinner reservations."

"The fact that you won't let yourself must be what's driving you crazy." She fanned her hands across his abdomen, nails digging into his muscles. "I'm not driving you crazy. You're driving yourself crazy." Raising on tiptoe, she breathed in his ear. "Let yourself go, Sebastian."

Yesterday at the pool she'd made it clear she wanted him. He sure as hell wanted her. Telling himself he was keeping his distance to restore their relationship to a professional level had kept him from acting on his desire for her. But she'd hinted last night that she was close to accepting a job offer.

Once she was gone out of his life, how long before he would no longer be tortured by the longing to skim her curves and spend hours drifting kisses over her skin?

"I can't." He pulled her hands away and pinned them to the wall. "People are waiting for us."

"Typical."

"What does that mean?"

"You always do the right thing. The thing everyone expects."

"What's wrong with that?"

"It gets old pretty quick. I offered you a free pass for one night of uninhibited sex—sex without expectations of anything more—and it's as if the whole thing made your world a bad place to be. You need to loosen up and learn to have fun or you're going to miss out on all the wonderful things life has to offer." She drew a deep breath and kept going. "Everybody at Case Consolidated Holdings lives in terror of not being completely perfect. Have you ever wondered why we've had so much staff turnover in the last year? It's because working for you makes people crack up."

Had she just called him a tyrant? "You've survived for four years. It can't be that bad."

"Survived?" She stared down her nose at him, a monumental feat, considering he towered over her by at least eight inches. "Do you think surviving a job is something I should be grateful for?"

Perhaps not. "What do you suggest I do?"

"Well, for starters, you could lighten up. Have some fun. Stop trying to manage every single thing around you."

"I don't manage *everything*."

"You've scheduled the summit down to the minute."

"We have a lot to get through."

"Not at night, you don't."

"Part of what makes this summit work is that all the executives spend time together."

Missy rolled her eyes. "Right, but they're together all day."

Sebastian had worked with Missy long enough to know when she had a point to make. "What do you have in mind?"

"Cancel the group dinners and let everyone go their own way."

"It's too late for tonight's dinner."

"True." She nodded, her eyes shining. "But it would be a simple thing to cancel the rest of them. I know you'd make the wives very happy if you gave them more time alone with their husbands. With the amount of traveling you have got everyone doing, your executives don't get to see much of their wives or their families." Her gaze lifted no higher than his chin. "And about the tours…"

Raw impatience burned in his gut. "What about the tours?"

"No one wanted to go to the Hoover Dam."

"You didn't go?" Sebastian couldn't believe what he was hearing. This summit was coming apart. Not one thing had gone according to plan since he and Missy had stepped off the plane. "Dare I ask what you did instead?"

"We hit a couple casinos then I suggested they might like to try skydiving."

"Skydiving?"

"Oh, don't worry. It was indoor skydiving," she said in a breezy tone. "I wasn't out to get anyone killed. They found it fun rather than terrifying."

"Fun," Sebastian muttered. "Your idea?"

She looked surprised that he'd even asked. "Of course."

"Is there anything else I need to know?"

"Like what?"

"Oh, I don't know. Did you rearrange tomorrow's summit schedule without telling me?"

"Now that you mention it—" She broke off when he growled. Her laughter filled the suite and took the sting out of everything he'd just heard. "I'm kidding. I wouldn't dream of messing with your precious summit."

"Because, I'm assuming, you've already promised my agreement on the change of plans," he said. "Fine, I'll go along with it."

"That was too easy." For the first time she sounded concerned. "What did I miss?"

"The fact that from now until the end of the summit, you have seen to it that my nights are free."

"And?"

"So are yours."

"She almost started to cry today while we were shopping." Alicia Darby's voice lifted over the laughter bouncing off the glass walls separating their private dining room from the rest of the Eiffel Tower Restaurant.

"How can you call what you do shopping?" Missy protested.

"So, we found a nice quiet bar." Susan's eyes were dancing with mirth.

"We're calling her the one-drink wonder," Alicia said. "She's a lightweight."

Maggie Hambly jumped in. "No stamina."

"You have no idea how hard it is to keep these ladies happy," Missy protested, fluttering her hand in the direction of the wives.

"Oh, we know." Owen Darby looked to the other husbands. They were all nodding.

Missy sat back with a defeated sigh as the waiter cleared

her plate. Dinner had been a boisterous affair, driven by the wives' enthusiasm over the day's activities. She'd joined in when prompted, but for the most part she'd eaten in silence, her nerves on high alert.

Driven by a compulsion too strong to resist, her gaze sped down the table toward her boss. The sparks in his eyes reminded her of muzzle fire. He'd watched her all night, his intense scrutiny disturbing her equilibrium as effectively as if his hands were gliding along her skin.

Missy dropped her gaze to the elegant dessert the waiter placed before her. The dish was beautiful, but her stomach could no more handle the rich chocolate soufflé than the delicious sea bass in champagne brown butter broth she'd ordered.

Had he meant what she hoped when he'd pointed out that she'd freed up his nights and hers also? He'd gone all mysterious when she'd asked him to explain. She wasn't sure where they stood anymore.

Did he mean to spend the nights with her? In what capacity? As boss and employee? As lovers?

Anticipation shivered through her.

For two days she'd been longing to be in his arms again. Teasing Sebastian had been like playing with fire, but she wasn't worried about getting burned. Her boss had made it clear that while he might find her attractive, he intended to keep their relationship professional. Had that changed?

She had no idea how long she'd been lost in thought when the couples around her began to get up from the table. A warm hand grazed her shoulder. From the way her nerve endings perked up, she knew Sebastian stood behind her.

The room was clearing fast. Everyone was excited about the Cirque du Soleil show they were attending. Before she knew it, only she, Sebastian and his parents remained.

"Dad, you and Mom use our tickets for the show tonight."

Our tickets? Missy tipped her head back and stared at him in confusion. What did he mean?

"Are you sure?" his mother asked, her gaze bouncing from Sebastian to Missy.

"Absolutely." Sebastian slid his thumb along her nape. "I have some unfinished business I need to attend to."

Missy's stomach dipped and rolled at the subtext beneath his statement. Did his unfinished business involve her?

"Come, Missy. Let's get back to that matter we were discussing earlier."

Heat bloomed in her cheeks as she pushed back from the table. What had she gotten herself into? Did he really intend to work or was his mind occupied with the same carnal thoughts that had plagued her throughout dinner?

"What matter?" she muttered as they followed his parents out of the restaurant.

"The matter of your free time."

Well, that didn't tell her a darned thing. Dazed by the knowing glint in his eye, she gnawed her lower lip and joined his parents in the elevator.

While Susan exclaimed over the show they were about to see, Missy cast surreptitious glances at Sebastian's profile. The third time she looked his way, his eyes snagged hers. One dark eyebrow twitched, telling her he knew his ambiguous response was driving her crazy.

Missy shifted her attention to the wall beside him until the elevator doors opened. The heat of his hand on the small of her back further knotted her emotions and her pulse skittered like a nervous mouse as they bid the group of executives and wives goodbye and settled into a taxi for the ride back to the hotel.

She stared out the window at the millions of lights that set the strip ablaze and wondered what was going through his mind.

As the cab drew up to the hotel, she summoned the nerve to find out. "Do you really intend to work?"

The shadows inside the cab masked his expression. "No."

"Then what are we going to do?"

The taxi stopped beneath the hotel's canopy. Sebastian paid the driver and slid out. Missy took the hand he extended and let him pull her from the cab.

"I thought I'd leave that up to you."

She trembled at the husky rumble of his voice. Putting the ball in her court gave her control over what happened in the next few hours. She knew what she wanted. Another night of heaven in Sebastian's arms. Isn't it what she'd been lobbying for? He probably expected her to suggest they run up to the suite and hop into bed.

Not a bad idea, really.

"Why let me decide?"

"You said I'm too hung up on being in control so I'm handing you the power." He let go of her hand and slid his hands into his pockets. His watchful gaze sent shivers up her spine. "So, what's it going to be, Missy?"

Sebastian tensed as he awaited her answer. Around them, bellhops and hotel guests faded from his awareness. His entire being was focused on Missy and the parade of emotions across her beautiful face.

Eyelashes casting shadows on her cheeks, she nibbled on her lower lip while a smile played with the corners of her mouth. Thousands of lights blazed above them, highlighting the bright spots of color in her cheeks. Her body language spoke of indecision. Now that he'd taken a step down that path, she was hesitating?

"Feel like taking my new car for a spin?"

From her tiny clutch she'd produced a set of keys. Sebastian stared at them without comprehension. While he'd been pondering the joys of taking her naked body for a spin, she'd had another sort of ride in mind.

"What new car?"

"The one I won earlier today."

Humor dimmed the roar of his libido. "You won a car?" He shook his head. "Of course, you did. It seems you've come to Vegas to break the bank."

"Where else can a girl get lucky?" she quizzed, peering at him from beneath her lashes.

Sebastian let the double entendre pass by without comment. "Lead the way."

Half an hour later, they'd cleared the lights of Las Vegas and headed north and west into the mountains. Missy drove. She'd been surprised that he'd insisted she get behind the wheel and seeing his broad grin, she was pleased he had.

She'd hiked the hem of her snug dress to mid thigh. Given that she'd bared more at the pool yesterday, he shouldn't be enjoying the view as much as he was. A couple of hair clips, scrounged from her purse, kept her fiery locks from whipping in the wind, but a few tendrils had escaped her top knot and blew about her cheeks.

"You're looking pretty relaxed over there," she remarked.

"Any reason why I shouldn't be?"

"I'm doing a hundred and ten miles an hour."

He was unfazed by the dangerous speed. His only anxiety involved how much of the night this wild ride would eat up. He wanted to get her alone and naked as soon as possible to take advantage of the exhilaration that gripped her.

"Do you want me to slow down?"

"You're in charge tonight, remember? I'm at your mercy."

The wind snatched away the disparaging sound she made, but he had little trouble reading her skepticism in the fading light.

The sky had lost any tinge of red as they'd reached the outskirts of Las Vegas. Stars appeared as cobalt then became navy. Sebastian let his head fall backward and stared at the vast space that surrounded them. Leaving behind the frantic energy of Vegas was like stepping into a rain forest. Peace filled him.

A reduction in the car's vibration told him she'd eased off the accelerator. The world continued to streak by, but he could pick out a few more details in the shadowy landscape.

"Are you sure you don't want to drive?"

"Positive." He turned his head in her direction. "Being your passenger lets me enjoy the view."

Her gaze left the road and darted his direction. "Except you're not looking at the scenery. You're staring at me."

"Exactly."

She returned her attention to the empty two-lane road. "I don't get it." Her lopsided smile told a different story. She liked his attention.

"Don't get what?"

"Why'd you leave your dad in charge of entertaining the executives tonight?"

"Rather odd for a control freak like me, isn't it?"

"Are you planning on throwing that in my face all night?"

"I don't know. Are we going to spend the night together?"

"I hadn't given it much thought." Missy's breathless tone gave her away.

Sebastian grinned. "I have no plans in case you're wondering." He noted the time on the dashboard clock. Nine-thirty. They'd been driving an hour. "We can drive all night if that's what you want."

"But what do you want to do?"

"I'm not the one in charge of tonight's entertainment. You are."

The car slowed still more. "I don't like being in charge."

"Really? I'm enjoying it immensely."

The car stopped. Missy made a U-turn and began to head back to town. Sebastian hid his relief.

"Why?"

"Because role reversal is a good way to broaden your understanding of someone else."

"And that's what we're doing?" she prompted, her tone wry. "Broadening our understanding of each other?"

"You tell me. How does it feel to be in charge of all the decisions?"

"Exhausting. How do you do it all the time?"

He laughed. "It's not so bad once you get used to it. And I don't make all the decisions all the time. Why do you think I gave you my house to decorate?"

"When did you become so enlightened?"

"Around the time you called me a tyrant, I think."

She shook her head. "I never called you a tyrant."

"You told me my demanding ways were responsible for the company's employee turnover. If that's true, I'm not acting like a good leader, am I? And that's what this week is all about—improving leadership skills."

"I forgot to ask you how it went today. Is your father behaving himself?"

Sebastian entertained Missy with stories of his father's preoccupation with his cell phone as they drove back to the hotel.

"I'm surprised," she said as the lights of Las Vegas drew closer. "He seemed very interested in your speech."

"When did you talk to him about that?"

"This morning as I was checking to make sure everything was ready to go."

Sebastian drummed his fingers on the car door. "What else did you talk about?"

She must have heard the tension in his voice because she grimaced. "Nothing about what he saw in your suite yesterday morning, if that's what you're worried about."

"I wasn't," he lied.

Conversation drifted into less complicated topics as she

negotiated the strip and parked the car back at the hotel. He set his hand on the small of her back as he guided her across the concrete to the elevator that would return them to the hotel's lobby. From there they could head into the casino or back to his suite. He wondered which she'd choose.

"Winning the car was fun," Missy said as they stepped of the elevator and were met by the activity of a casino in full swing. "Problem is, I don't know how to get it home."

Sebastian followed her as they headed toward the elevators that serviced the hotel's rooms. Tension leaked out of his body with each step. She was obviously not interested in gambling away the night. But was she up for anything else?

"Max ships cars all the time," he said. "I'll give him a call in the morning and see if he has a carrier he can recommend."

"I never thought about shipping it home. I figured I'd either have to drive it back to Texas or sell it before I left."

The elevator deposited them on their floor. Sebastian kept his hands to himself as they walked down the hall. He didn't trust himself to touch her. Plus, he'd put her in charge of tonight's entertainment. She was in control.

"Why would you sell it?"

"I've never owned anything so impractical before."

"Maybe it's time that changed."

They stopped beside the door to her hotel room. Missy regarded him with open curiosity, waiting to see what he'd do. Sebastian surveyed the pliant curves of her mouth.

"Good night, Missy," he said, squashing his satisfaction at her disappointed expression. Whether they spent the night together was her decision to make. He bent down and brushed his lips across her cheek, lingering to enjoy her tantalizing fragrance. "Sweet dreams."

With her disappointment in Sebastian's chaste kiss thundering through her body, Missy watched him disappear into his hotel suite, leaving her abandoned in the empty hall. Heat blasted her cheeks. Her hands trembled so badly she had trouble fitting the keycard into the slot. She stumbled through the door when it opened, scarcely supported by knees turned to warm jelly. The bed looked like a safe place to rest until the whirling in her head slowed. Instead, she walked to the door that connected her room to Sebastian's.

When she pulled it open, she found him waiting for her. Before she completed her sigh of relief, he'd caught her up in his arms and strode toward the bedroom.

"Hey," she protested. "I thought I was in charge of tonight's activities."

"As soon as I get you naked I'm at your command."

Sebastian dispatched her dress with more urgency than finesse. She wasn't wearing stockings, but he made quick work of her bra and panties.

"Beautiful," he murmured, his lips drifting down her neck. He lowered her to the bed, ignoring his earlier promise to let her be in charge.

Missy didn't care. She tugged his coat off his broad shoulders and somehow worked all his shirt buttons free.

"Help me," she demanded as her fingers fumbled with his belt.

Brushing her hands aside, he rolled off the bed and shed the rest of his clothes. Gloriously naked and aroused, he returned to her.

"Fast or slow?" he queried, his tongue dipping into her navel.

Missy's hips bucked off the mattress as his fingers glided up her thigh. "Yes."

He chuckled. "It can't be both. That was an either-or question."

"Shut up and kiss me."

"That I can do."

And to her delight he did.

Long, slow and deep. Tender and adoring. By the time

Sebastian settled between her thighs, his kisses and caresses had touched every inch of her skin.

"I could get used to this," she sighed as his erection nudged her entrance. She clutched his shoulders as he flexed his hips and drove home.

He framed her face with his hands and smiled. "Get used to what?"

As he began to move, Missy arched her back to take him deeper, the sense of fulfillment touching every cell in her body. She belonged to him. And he to her. They were a match. No wonder she'd lasted longer than any other assistant he'd had. She understood him like no one ever had before.

She could get used to having his arms around her every day. Get used to arguing with him as often as they made love. Get used to being the woman he came home to every day.

"I could get used to telling you what to do."

Seven

A good three feet separated Missy from the floor-to-ceiling windows in Sebastian's suite and the fifteen-story drop to the bright lights of the Vegas strip. The view enthralled her, but the height made her head spin. Seemed like a lot of things made her head spin since she'd come to this glitzy city. The man sleeping in the bed behind her was the leading cause.

"What are you doing?" A large hand cupped her upper arm while his other one brushed aside her hair so he could place a warm, compelling kiss on the spot where her neck and shoulder came together.

She leaned back against his warm muscles and sighed. "Looking at the view. It's beautiful."

"Why so far from the windows?"

"It's silly but I'm a little nervous about heights ever since my brother Matt scared me into thinking he was going to push me from the bell tower of our church."

Those sexy, persuasive lips coasted along her bare shoulder. "Why would he do that?"

"Because he was twelve and thought it was funny."

"How old were you?" His fingertips slipped along the edge

of her bra and ghosted around her nipple. It peaked against the fabric as a bolt of sensation shot to her core.

"Six."

"I remember being mischievous at that age, but I don't recall tormenting little girls half my age."

"You didn't have sisters," she reminded him, losing herself in the sensual fog that filled her mind whenever his hands were on her.

"Why are you wearing this?"

The straps of her bra slipped down her arms as he unhooked it. Missy pressed her hands to her chest, catching the flimsy material to preserve her wits.

"I was heading back to my room."

"But the night is still young."

He coaxed her to give up the bra and palmed her breasts, kneading the tender flesh and rolling her nipples between his fingers until she gasped and closed her eyes. The rest of her senses sprang to life.

Before she knew it, her underwear had pooled at her feet. He raised her arms above her head, arching her back against his torso. He stroked his hands over her breasts, across her stomach and down toward the triangle of hair at the apex of her thighs. She buried her fingers in his hair and parted for him, a moan escaping her lips as he pressed the heel of his hand against her mound.

He found her ultra-sensitive bud and circled it with his index finger. "That's it, let it happen."

Missy shuddered as he fondled her, breathing Sebastian's name as she surrendered to his mastery. Her lips parted as meaningless words of encouragement poured out of her, and she felt herself start to unravel as he slid his finger up inside of her. He dragged kisses down the side of her neck, teeth nipping at the cord of her throat. Her body jerked in response, cueing the explosion that erupted like a series of deep shock waves through her.

Limp as a noodle in the aftermath, she appreciated the support of Sebastian, solid and steady against her back. In that second, she knew she could face her worst fears with his arms around her.

Spinning out of his arms, she caught him by the hand and backed toward the windows.

"What are you doing?" he asked, his free hand cupping her cheek.

"Facing my fear." Her peripheral vision filled with bright lights and empty space. A familiar anxiety tightened like a band around her chest. She shoved the panic down and ran her hand along Sebastian's bicep. The muscles in his chest flexed as her fingers traced his powerful contours. Appreciation purred through her. "Feel like helping me?"

"What did you have in mind?"

"I was hoping you could replace my negative memory of heights with a positive one." She continued to move backward until there was nowhere to go. A gasp escaped her as she realized nothing stood between her and a fifteen-story drop but inch-thick glass.

The arms Sebastian slid around her tensed as if he was ready to pull her to safety at the first sign of trouble.

She concentrated on Sebastian's strength and concern, refusing to be ruled by fear. The sensation of chilly glass against her back and hot male against her breasts and stomach was far more powerful than any phobia.

"Are you sure this is a good idea?"

"It will be if you make the memory sensational."

The lips that grazed hers wore a smile. "I can do that."

She felt the urgent bite of his hands on her hips and butt as he trailed his tongue across her lower lip. She grabbed fistfuls of his hair and pushed up on tiptoe as his mouth seized hers, stealing the air from her lungs before sharing his breath with her.

Urgent, wordless moans erupted from her throat as he

lifted her off her feet. She clutched his shoulders, legs parting wide, and wrapped her thighs around his hips as he settled her onto his engorged shaft. They both growled in appreciation at the snug fit of their bodies.

Sebastian rocked against her powerfully, driving her pleasure higher. Missy held on to him for dear life and wondered at the strength of the passion between them. How could he make her so wild with so little effort?

Astonished to feel another surging orgasm ripping through her, Missy called his name and heard Sebastian groan in masculine appreciation. He drove deep into her, his hips pulsing frantically as he neared his own completion. While wave after wave of sensation rolled through her, Sebastian's fingers bit down hard on her hips as he came.

He sagged against her, pinning her to the window. The drop that had terrified her moments before now filled her with delight. She might not be ready to go bungee jumping or skydiving, but she'd make love with Sebastian in a skyscraper anytime.

He stroked the hair from her face and bussed her cheek. "How was that?"

"Fabulous," she retorted weakly, leaning her head back against the glass. "Thanks to you, I'm now a fan of heights."

"Glad I could help." His voice soft with amusement, he kissed her temple. "Give me a second and I'll put you down."

"Don't hurry on my account. I'm quite comfortable." She tightened her inner muscles around him and he shuddered. If she'd been able to see his expression, Missy knew for certain it would make her grin.

Her heartbeat had almost returned to normal by the time he eased free of her body and set her back on her feet.

"Come back to bed." He towered over her.

"I really have to go," she began. Her proclamation ended in a sharp cry as he hoisted her off her feet and carried her back to bed fireman style.

"Stay a while longer. I'll make it worth your while."

"Worth my while?" Missy rolled onto her stomach, a mild but satisfying ache in every muscle, and buried her face in the mattress. "I don't think I can take much more."

"Oh, you might be surprised," he said, joining her on the bed. "We'll rest a while and then see how you're feeling."

He sounded so pleased with himself she picked up her head to scold. "You are completely insatiable."

"I'm insatiable?" He settled on his back beside her, hands behind his head, and smirked. "Who's been having orgasms at the drop of a hat?"

Kicking her feet in the air, she threaded the sheets between her fingers. "So you're a great lover. Quit bragging."

"I don't think it has anything to do with my skills." He leaned over for a quick kiss. "I think we have great chemistry."

"For another four days," she reminded him. "Then, it's back to Houston and what happened in Vegas…"

"Stays in Vegas." Suddenly serious, he took her hand and kissed her palm. "What if I don't want it to end?"

She froze. Her entire body flushed hot, then cold. Goose bumps broke out on her skin. "It has to."

"Does it? Until two days ago, you've had a knack of keeping me on track and calm."

"And now?"

"You drive me crazy. And I don't care." One side of Sebastian's mouth kicked up. "I'm not ready to lose you."

The predatory glint in his gray eyes warned her some shift in their dynamic had happened.

"I'm not sure I understand what you mean."

"Then let me be clear." A soft light entered his eyes. "One night was not enough. A week is not enough. I want more."

Her heart stopped beating. She'd had no expectations when she'd wagered one night with Sebastian. But a connection had been made. Hearing him reveal that he, too, felt it made her heart sing.

"More?" A second week? A month? "How much more?"

"Do we have to define it?"

Anxious buzzing began in the back of her mind. "I'd like some idea what you have in mind."

"Let's start slow and see where it goes."

Start slow and soon she'd be making plans. She wouldn't mean to. It was just something that happened in her psyche. She'd been saving for two years to buy a wedding dress. She wanted to get married. And deep down, where she knew better than to look, she suspected she wanted to marry Sebastian.

Missy shook her head. This thing between them was about passion. Like her high school boyfriend, Sebastian had just seen something he wanted and taken it when the opportunity arose. And as with her high school boyfriend, eventually their differences would drive them apart.

"Where do you want it to go?" Despite every sensible thought in her head, hope made her heart dance. She squashed the emotion. Sebastian didn't want to date her. This went against everything she'd been telling herself to expect from him.

"I have no expectations," he said. "No need to control the outcome. Let's see where it takes us."

"And my job as your assistant?"

"Can I convince you to stay on?"

"No."

He nodded as if he'd expected that answer. "You've been a part of my life for years. I'm not ready to let you go quite yet."

Sebastian's desire for her might be real, but she knew it wasn't something that would last once they returned home. Unfortunately, she was already half in love with him. Any more time in his arms was going to make it impossible to walk away.

"And when you're done with me? What then?"

"Aren't you being a bit dramatic?" His lips tightened. "I should probably warn you that Chandra overplayed her hand all too often. I don't like it."

He rarely talked about his ex-wife, but from his mother, Missy knew Chandra had been a handful. "I'm not being dramatic—just trying to figure out what's in it for me."

"After tonight, I would think that would be obvious."

If he'd offered her something besides fabulous sex, she'd have melted like butter on a hot skillet. Annoyed by his unromantic pitch, she scowled. "I suppose you think that's the sort of offer I'd jump at."

"What do you want?"

His question startled her. Sebastian had fulfilled all her fantasies and introduced a few new ones.

"I don't want anything."

"That's not true. Everyone wants something."

"Not me." Nothing she was willing to admit to him, anyway.

"You have me in the palm of your hand." Turning her hand palm up, he rubbed his thumb along her lifeline until her entire body began to tingle. "This would be a great time to tell me what would make you happy."

She shook her head, her heart in her throat. "You really do suck at negotiating."

"I like to think of myself as direct."

"I don't want anything more than what I have right here and now." To expect anything more would only lead to heartbreak. "The rest of the week together and then we go our separate ways."

"Unacceptable."

Before she could protest, her purse began to ring. Like

Pavlov's dog, she was conditioned to react to a familiar sound, only instead of drooling, she sat up.

"Leave it," Sebastian commanded, tugging her back down.

She squirmed out of his grasp. "It's not you calling so it must be important."

"Very funny." He rolled onto his side and watched her cross the room to the dresser.

The phone had stopped ringing by the time she fished it out of her purse. "Whoever it was, I missed the call."

"Come back to bed."

"Just a second, let me check my messages." Something about the late-night call gnawed at her nerves. No one except Sebastian would call her at such an hour. That meant something was wrong. When her brother's voice sounded in her ear, she knew she was right.

"Missy, when you get this, call me. Dad's been hurt. We're heading to the hospital now." Heart twisting in fear, she ended the message and turned to face Sebastian.

He came off the bed in time to catch her as she swayed. "What's wrong?"

"Sam left me a message. He said my dad's been hurt. They're heading to the hospital."

"Call him back and see what happened."

Her hands shook so badly, it took her three tries before she keyed up her address book and found her brother's cell phone number. Not until the phone started ringing did it occur to her that she could have just found his missed call and hit send. Sebastian wrapped her in a robe and rubbed her arms while she waited for her brother to pick up.

"Missy, it's bad," Sam said.

"What happened?"

"He was stabbed."

"Stabbed?" Her gaze found Sebastian's. She caught concern reflected there. His fingers tightened. "How did that happen?"

"I don't have a lot of details. There'll probably be more once we get to the hospital and talk to the cops."

"Is he going to be okay?"

"He's a tough old bird."

She squeezed her eyes shut and counted to five. "I'm going to catch the first plane out of here."

"Aren't you in Vegas at that thing for your company?"

"Yes, but Sebastian will understand that I have to leave."

He leaned forward and kissed her on the temple. The tender caress brought a lump to her throat. She sank into his strength, letting him absorb some of her trembling.

"I'll keep you informed as we get news."

The hand holding the phone dropped to her side. "My dad's been hurt. I have to go home."

"Let me take care of everything. You go pack."

Numb, she got to her feet and stumbled out of the bedroom. She tossed clothes and toiletries into her suitcase and dressed in jeans and a T-shirt. Zipping her bag, she slid her feet into sandals.

Sebastian entered her room. He wore slacks and a dress shirt. "I have a plane waiting to take us back to Texas."

"Us?" She couldn't be processing his words properly.

"You don't seriously think I'm going to let you go by yourself, do you?" He took charge of her suitcase and wrapped strong fingers around her elbow to escort her into the hall.

"But what about the summit? And your meeting with Smythe tomorrow? You can't disappear at such a crucial time."

"I guess it's good that my dad showed up, isn't it?"

They stepped onto the elevator and Sebastian pushed the button for the lobby. Missy shivered as reaction settled in. Sebastian pulled her into his arms and shared his heat with her.

"You're chilled. Do you have a coat?"

She shook her head. "I tossed everything out. Remember?"

He bought her a sweatshirt at the hotel gift shop and

dressed her in it as if she were a small child. Caught in a dark place, Missy let him lead her across the lobby and get them into a cab. Tucked into the crook of his arm, she huddled against his side as she watched the Las Vegas strip slide by the car window.

They boarded a private plane and were taxiing down the runway as the sky began to lighten over Las Vegas. As the city lights fell behind them, Missy began to disengage from the fantasy of the last few days.

Sleeping with Sebastian a couple times might not be a mistake, but letting herself fall for a man who never intended to marry her went against her solemn vow to never again let herself reach too high. If she hadn't let her heart lead, she never would have begun a game she could never hope to survive, much less win.

Missy put her hands between her thighs, all too conscious of Sebastian's shoulder a few tempting inches away. It was more than wonderful of him to worry about her comfort. To arrange for a plane to take her to Crusade. To sit beside her the whole way there. This sort of behavior made a girl want to rely on him. To lose herself in his strong arms and let him soothe her fears.

And then what?

When they returned to Houston, she wouldn't be his employee or his lover. She wouldn't be anything.

It was better to disengage now. Before she became too dependent on a dream.

His hand covered her forearm, the firm pressure bringing a lump to her throat. She told herself the sympathetic gesture was one anyone would make. She'd seen her mother offer support in a similar manner.

Her heart squeezed. What did she expect? That he'd fall madly in love with her in the space of a few days? She pressed her lips together and shot a tight smile his way.

"Your father's going to be fine."

"I hope so." Worrying about her love life while her father's life hung in the balance demonstrated what a selfish idiot she was. "Thank you for everything."

"You don't need to thank me."

But she did. He'd left Las Vegas in the middle of his leadership summit to be there for her. He'd gone above and beyond the call of duty. And she wanted to make more of his motives than was wise.

"Sebastian." She struggled with how best to frame what she needed to say next. "I'd prefer it if my family didn't know anything about what happened between us in Las Vegas. I haven't told them that I broke up with Tim yet and…"

"You'd rather not further complicate an already complicated day."

"Yes." Although she was glad he understood, she couldn't help but wonder if he was relieved she wouldn't expect anything more from him.

An hour later, the plane landed at a small airstrip outside her hometown. She'd called Sam from the air and let him know what time they'd be landing. David was waiting as the sky began to lighten in the east. She hugged the youngest of her big brothers, clinging to him without asking how their father was doing, afraid the news had changed for the worse in the past two hours.

"Sebastian, this is my brother David."

The two men shook hands. David assessed Sebastian through narrowed eyes. Missy had spoken of her boss often, some of it not particularly flattering. She'd never expected him to meet anyone in her family.

"Thanks for bringing my sister. Dad's out of surgery, but he's still listed as critical."

They followed David to his truck. He tossed Missy's suitcase in the back. She sat between the men, staring out the windshield.

"What happened?" she demanded.

"We're not exactly sure. We think he got a call from Angela Ramirez's son. Her ex-boyfriend showed up drunk and half out of his mind. Dad went over there and tried to calm the guy down. He got stabbed."

"Why didn't he call the police?" she asked, ticking off familiar landmarks as they slid by in pre-dawn light.

"I think Angela Ramirez is here illegally."

"And Dad thought nothing of his own safety," Missy grumbled. "He was only worried that a member of his congregation was in trouble."

Beside her, Sebastian tensed. "Congregation?"

She'd never told her boss about her family or her upbringing and he'd never inquired about her past. Hopefully that wasn't about to blow up in her face.

"Didn't Missy tell you?" David piped up. "Our dad's a pastor."

Eight

Rarely was Sebastian struck dumb.

Missy was a preacher's daughter? How had she worked for him for four years and not shared that bit of news? Did he know her at all?

Unbidden, doubts rushed in. He'd known very little about Chandra before letting his passion get the better of him, and look how that had turned out. Her supposedly pregnant. Them married. Him discovering her lies and manipulation.

Now history was repeating itself with Missy. With her sexy curves and knack for shattering his restraint, she'd ignited his desire, made him lose control, and once again, he'd moved too fast.

Sebastian rubbed his cheek, hearing the rasp of stubble. He'd left without packing a bag, figuring he'd accompany Missy to the hospital, find out how her father was doing and then leave her in her family's care. Now he wished he'd never gotten on the plane in Las Vegas and never found out this tidbit about her origins.

"No," he said, rediscovering his voice. "She never mentioned that."

From the way she stared straight ahead, her eyes fixed on the road before them, he figured she had a pretty good idea how frustrated he was at the moment. He couldn't wait to get her alone so he could hear her reasons for keeping him in the dark.

Or did the blame lie at his feet?

How come he'd never asked about her family? Pressed her for details about growing up in west Texas. He'd taken and taken. Her free time. Her loyalty. Her expertise. And he couldn't even remember her birthday. Missy deserved better.

He glanced her way. Her fixed gaze and frozen expression confirmed that she wasn't happy. He rubbed his forehead.

"I'm not surprised," David said, appearing unaware of the tension that filled the pickup's cab. "She never acted like one growing up."

"I can't wait to hear all about it," Sebastian said.

"Wild." David slapped the steering wheel. "That's the best way to describe my sister."

"That's just not true," Missy protested. "I didn't act any different than any of my classmates."

"Oh, I don't know. You pushed things pretty far."

"That surprises me," Sebastian said. "She certainly doesn't give the appearance of someone with a checkered past."

"Checkered?" Missy shot him a warning look. "I'd hardly call staying out past curfew and drinking with my friends worthy of being called a checkered past. It was all the regular stuff teenagers get into."

"No stealing cars to go joyriding?"

"No."

"There was that time you and Jimmy McCray got stopped coming back from the lake."

"That was his mom's car. He didn't steal it. Just took it without mentioning it to her and she thought it had been stolen."

"That's probably because he was grounded and so were

you. Neither one of you was supposed to be out at three in the morning. And you sure weren't supposed to be doing whatever it was you two did down by the lake." David wore a wicked grin. "But you can't really stop young love, can you? Hey!" David exhaled air on a protest as his sister jabbed her elbow into his ribs.

"Shut up, David. You weren't exactly the poster child for upright behavior, either, when you were young. Chet's going to be eleven in five months. Maybe I should tell him about the time you stuck fireworks in a dead squirrel and blew it up on the back porch. I don't think you could sit down for a week after Dad found out." Missy paused for only a second before continuing. "Or, how about the time you and our trusty brother Matt—"

David's voice rose over hers. "Okay, I get your point, I'll shut up."

"Thank you." She smirked, but her pleased expression didn't last long.

Sebastian spoke softly in her ear. "I see we'll have lots to discuss when you get back to Houston."

She eyed him without turning her head. "It was a long time ago."

"But it's part of who you are so I'm interested in hearing all about it."

Like all small towns at five in the morning, Main Street looked buttoned up tight. David blew past five blocks of storefronts before Sebastian had a chance to blink. What had it been like for Missy to grow up in such a place? He'd guessed her hometown was small, but he had no idea how isolated. He'd assumed as a preacher's daughter, she wouldn't have had a lot of chances to learn how the world worked. Now, however, Sebastian recognized signs of the teenage rebel lurking beneath the sensible, efficient exterior of the woman who'd been his assistant for the past four years.

The truck passed a sign pointing the way to the hospital

and David took a right at the stoplight. Conversation suspended as David turned into the front driveway that would take them to the entrance.

"I'll drop you off here and park. Dad's probably still in recovery so everyone should be in the waiting room."

Sebastian slid out of the pickup and reached for Missy's hand to help her down. Despite the warm night and the sweatshirt she still wore, her hands were like ice. Shock. He recognized the signs. His mother had been like this when Brandon had collapsed. Sebastian knew what to do, offer a strong shoulder to lean on and keep the Kleenex coming. His mother had gone through an entire box before her husband had come out of triple bypass surgery.

Pulling Missy's arm through his, he tucked her hands between his arm and his body to warm her. She moved like a zombie at his side, her steps jerky as if her muscles had stopped functioning properly.

"It's going to be okay," he murmured as the hospital doors swung open before them.

They stepped over the threshold. Missy straightened her shoulders and pulled away. As hard as it was to let her go, Sebastian held back as Missy reunited with her family. Three tall men, mirror images of David, gathered her into tight hugs that left her teary and out of breath. Four women hovered behind the men, then took their turns, each returning to offer support to one of Missy's brothers.

With the greetings complete, Missy cast about for him. Sebastian's heart bumped against his ribs as her shell-shocked gaze found him. He came to her side, needing to wrap her in his arms, but she sensed his intention and shook her head, eyes pleading.

Turning to the group, she said, "Everyone. This is my boss, Sebastian Case."

As he shook hands with Missy's brothers, he couldn't help but contrast this tight group of brothers and wives with his own family. He and Max were close in age and the best of friends growing up, but as adults they'd gone out of state to different universities and taken different career paths. Eventually those paths had converged at Case Consolidated Holdings, but the years of separation had taken their toll. They'd become less like family and more like coworkers.

From what he gathered, Missy's family all lived within a couple miles of each other. In a few short minutes, he learned each brother was married and had between one and five kids ranging in ages from four months to fourteen years. He visualized boisterous family dinners every week with tons of children running around, and he understood why hitting thirty had heightened Missy's longing for marriage and children.

Two hours after they arrived, Reverend Ward was released to the ICU where he would be watched and monitored. Each of his children got to visit him one at a time. Missy went first, then sat beside Sebastian on a molded plastic chair, hands in her lap, distanced from him by her need to keep her family in the dark about their altered relationship.

He wasn't accustomed to seeing his ultra-efficient assistant so down and out. The sight unnerved him. Being unable to offer her support frustrated him. As she'd pointed out often these past couple days, he wasn't the sort to sit idle. He needed to help.

But he also needed to be in Las Vegas at the summit. Leaving his father in charge for more than a day could spell trouble.

At eight o'clock, he could wait no longer to check in. Not wanting to disturb Missy's family, he stood. Missy had closed her eyes and let her head fall back against the wall behind her. When he moved, she straightened and blinked in blurry disorientation. Rubbing her eyes, she looked around. The sisters-in-law had gone home to check on their children. All who remained were Missy's brothers.

"I'm going to step out and see how the summit is going," he told her, giving her hand a squeeze.

The cellular reception at the hospital had prevented him from receiving any calls. However, two messages awaited him. The first one made him curse.

Damn it. What the hell was going on?

He dialed Max's cell and heard the frustration in his brother's voice when he answered.

"Sebastian, I've been trying you for hours. Where've you been?"

"In Crusade with Missy. Her father was in an accident." No need to explain more. "Lucas Smythe said he's leaving the summit. What's going on?"

"He's not selling us his company." Despite the fact that this was an overseas call, Max's tension came through loud and clear.

Curses reverberated through Sebastian's head. "Why not?"

"Said he's having second thoughts."

"He was completely on board a week ago." What had their father said during a round of golf to convince Lucas that selling to them was a bad idea—or was getting caught with a half-naked Missy in his suite to blame? "Did he say what he's going to do instead?"

"No. He's heading home this morning. You have to convince him to change his mind. I'm in Amsterdam at the moment. My flight won't get in for another twelve hours."

"Send Nathan."

"Nathan isn't on board with this deal."

"He's on board," Sebastian said.

"I'm not sure I trust him to convince Smythe to sell to us."

Max still had a chip on his shoulder where their half brother was concerned. Sebastian suspected it had more to do with being unable to forgive their father for his infidelity than any animosity he felt toward Nathan.

Sebastian sighed. Early on, he'd had his doubts about being

able to work with Nathan; but lately their half brother had demonstrated that even though he might not be keen on the current business strategy for Case Consolidated Holdings, he was open to working with it.

"I won't make it back to Vegas before he leaves." Sebastian's gaze traveled across the waiting room to where Missy sat beside her brother.

"Fly to Raleigh and talk to him there."

An ache formed in Sebastian's chest as Missy rested her head on David's shoulder. She hadn't been willing to take comfort from him.

"Fine. I'll go." Sebastian ended the call without waiting for his brother's response.

He banked his fury at this unwelcome turn of events and headed toward Missy.

She'd been watching him the whole time and offered a weak smile as he neared. "Usually that would be me looking for you." She checked her watch. "It's almost eight in the morning. What's the crisis?"

"I have to fly to Raleigh. Lucas is backing out of our deal."

"Go," she said, nodding. "That's important."

More important than her. He read her loud and clear.

"I don't want to leave you."

She offered him a grateful smile. "I'll be okay. Dad's not out of danger, but the doctors think he'll make a full recovery. Smythe Industries is important." She got to her feet and tugged at his arm. "Come on. David can drive you back to the plane."

He was startled by how reluctant he was to leave her. For the first time in his life, he had no desire to return to work. Someone else should be able to take care of business, leaving him free to be with Missy a while longer. But that's not the way Case Consolidated Holdings was structured. His need to control all aspects of the business had made it so that he was the one who stepped in when things weren't working.

"You're sure you don't need me to stay?"

She shook off the scared, lost girl she'd been for the last few hours. Her spine straightened. She firmed her lips and enfolded herself in the brisk professionalism she usually demonstrated.

The transformation caught him off guard.

How often had she hidden hurt, fear or sadness from him? He'd taken her efficiency for granted, he saw now. She wasn't made of granite. Far from it.

He cupped her face in his hands. "Tell me you need me and I won't go."

Tears brightened her eyes. Her breath caught. She blinked a few times and swallowed hard. "That's not necessary. I have all my family here. I'll be fine."

"I don't doubt that. You're all wonderful support for each other. I just feel funny leaving you behind."

In truth, he'd gotten used to having her around all the time. Except for a half-dozen business trips that had lasted a week, he realized that he hadn't gone without seeing her for more than three days.

"You feel funny?" she echoed, a grin ghosting through her eyes.

And that was all it took. He leaned down and kissed her, not caring one single bit who saw.

Sebastian registered her utter shock before the compelling warmth of her soft lips made him forget everything but the way she made him feel. He wrapped his arms around her. With her fingers threaded through his hair, he savored the texture of her lips and the sweetness of her soft body.

A throat cleared behind him. "We should probably get going," David said.

Releasing her took longer than it should have. How long until he held her again? He knew she needed to be here for her dad and family. But he'd been a selfish bastard for so long and couldn't resist hoping that she was back in Houston within a couple weeks.

With her cheeks a bright pink she peered at him from beneath her lashes. "If it's okay with you, I'm going to stick around for a while."

His instincts screamed that leaving her here was a bad idea, but what could he do? Her family needed her. His company needed him.

"Take as much time as you need."

Just come back to me.

"I'm doing fine," Malcolm Ward said, pushing away Missy's attempt at dinner. "Don't you think it's time you went back to Houston? It's been three weeks."

Missy stopped dragging her fork through the lumpy mashed potatoes and met her father's gaze. She hadn't told him she'd quit her job. He needed to focus on his recovery. If he had any idea she had no pressing reason to return to Houston, he'd start worrying about her instead of getting better. Not that her dad was any good at thinking about himself. Always, his congregation came first. Then his family. Then the rest of the world. Then himself.

Having a saint for a father had never been easy.

"I have over a month of vacation saved up. Sebastian doesn't have any problem with me using it to take care of you."

"How much time do you have left?"

Three days.

"Plenty."

She carried her plate to the sink and dumped the burnt meatloaf and overcooked green beans into the garbage disposal. Normally her father protested any waste, but not even he would wish that dinner on anyone.

"Who's filling in for you while you're gone?"

"They hired a temp. It's done all the time. Don't worry.

There'll be a job for me when I go back." Someone would hire her. Or she could stay at Case Consolidated Holdings as the director of communications. If the position was still available.

"Your brothers like him."

"Who?" She transferred a large slice of chocolate cake to a plate and set it before her father. Chocolate was one thing he let himself indulge in.

"Your boss."

"Sebastian is terrific." Thinking about him sent a sweet pain shooting through her body. During the three days her father had spent in the hospital, struggling to heal and overcome the infection that had kept him delirious, Missy hadn't had time to dwell on what had happened in Las Vegas or fuss over what the future might bring.

"Cares about you, does he?"

Missy sat down with her own wedge of triple chocolate delight. She couldn't cook, but she knew how to bake.

"I've worked for him a long time."

"From what I hear, there's more to it than that."

Her cheeks burned beneath her father's all-knowing stare. Who'd told him? David? She'd sworn him to secrecy. He wouldn't spill the beans for fear that she would tell his wife how much he paid for that new revolver.

"I have no idea what you mean."

"He's called here every day, sometimes twice a day."

"That's about work." She found little breathing room in the barrage of her father's questioning. "They've recently bought a new company." In her absence, Sebastian had saved the deal with Smythe Industries. "There are a lot of details involved in integrating their employees into Case Consolidated Holdings, and he's calling me to help the temp with contact information and such."

"And the kiss he gave you at the hospital?" her dad

quizzed, his tone conversational. "How were you planning on explaining that? Improved employer-employee relations?"

"Who told you?" Missy clapped her hands over her hot cheeks. She hadn't felt this embarrassed since her father had caught her and Wayne Stodemeyer necking in the tool shed when she was fifteen. "If it was David, I'll…" She let her threat trail off, unwilling to voice her intention to break one of the Ten Commandments to her dad the minister.

"Don't worry, your brother didn't rat you out. It was one of the nurses."

"Great. Just great."

"Is that why Tim broke up with you?" her father quizzed, revealing that his ability to know everything that went on around him wasn't quelled by the fact that he'd almost died three weeks ago.

Missy shoved aside that horrifying thought so she could deal with setting her father straight.

"No. Tim broke up with me because I worked too many hours and he was lonely. He found someone new. Sebastian had nothing to do with it."

Nothing directly. Although in the past few weeks she'd analyzed her relationship with Tim and come to see that her crush on Sebastian hadn't been as over as she'd assumed. It had interfered with her priorities.

"I see. Are you two a couple then?"

"Sebastian and me?" The words exploded out of her on an incredulous laugh. "Of course not. I'm not his type. If he ever gets married again, he's going to choose someone gorgeous, wealthy and sophisticated. Three things I'm not and never will be."

"Maybe you have it wrong."

Not possible. She'd seen the way he'd looked at her small town. He'd been polite to her family, but he'd also been sizing everyone up. She wouldn't trade a single brother, sister-in-law, niece or nephew for anyone from Sebastian's well-connected circle; but that didn't mean she was blind to their flaws or shortcomings.

None of her brothers had the sort of ambition that kept them working sixty hours a week at their jobs. The second oldest, Jacob, had taken until he was in his mid-thirties to figure out what he wanted to be when he grew up. They were college educated and had successful careers, but they balanced work with family.

Sebastian wouldn't recognize the value in balance. He'd chosen business over family.

"Do you have feelings for him?" her dad persisted, breaking into her thoughts.

"Of course. And he has feelings for me. Just not the same sort of feelings."

Or that's what she told herself. She really didn't have a clue what Sebastian wanted beyond her returning as his assistant—or her spending an indefinite amount of time in his bed. Back in Las Vegas, she'd doubted there was a future for them past Las Vegas. Now that he'd seen where she'd grown up, she doubted it even more.

If only she could get that goodbye kiss out of her head. The hungry strength in the arms around her. The way it seemed to take a long time for him to let go. She told herself not to read too much into his daily phone calls or the smooth caress of his tone as he asked her how she was doing.

She rubbed her arms as goose bumps appeared. Beneath her father's keen regard she finished her chocolate cake and went to start the dishes.

"Thanks for dinner," he said, his arms sliding around her from behind. He kissed her cheek. "I think you should go back to Houston. You can't hide out here forever."

Missy whirled on her father, a protest cocked and ready, but he was already out the door, moving better than he had since coming home from the hospital. He'd done that on purpose, hit her with a blunt opinion and then fled before she could defend herself.

Was she hiding?

Damn right she was hiding.

Almost four weeks ago she'd quit her job and slept with her boss. Returning to Houston meant having to cope with both things. She wasn't ready to decide on anything more taxing than whether to bake another chocolate cake or to shake things up and try lemon.

"I'm going to the store," she called, grabbing her purse and the keys to the truck.

"Can you pick up a prescription for me while you're out?" her father asked from the living room.

Missy made the drugstore her first stop. She could use a tube of toothpaste. All she'd packed before going to Las Vegas was travel-sized toiletries. A week ago she'd run out of her brand and started using her dad's and didn't like it at all. Another sign that she needed to go home.

Browsing the aisles, she added shampoo, lotion and dental floss to her basket. It wasn't until she passed the feminine products that she stopped cold. She'd been in town almost four weeks and in Las Vegas three days before that without having her period. Whipping out her phone, she keyed up her calendar and tracked backward.

She should have started two weeks ago. Either she'd skipped her period because she was stressed, or she was pregnant. How was that possible? She and Sebastian had been careful.

A wave of dizziness struck her. Except for that first time. They'd been so caught up in the moment neither one of them had thought about protection. But to get pregnant after one mistake? That just wasn't realistic.

She needed to find out for sure, and she needed to know tonight. But she couldn't buy the test here. Everyone would know. Her father would find out. She'd head over a couple towns and hit a pharmacy where no one would recognize her.

In a fog, Missy paid for her purchases and headed to the truck. Forty-five minutes later she sat in the bathroom of a roadside diner and checked her watch for the fifteenth time in thirty seconds.

She was waiting for a blue bar, but she didn't really need it. She'd convinced herself she was carrying Sebastian's child. Time rushed at her like a charging bull. Regret squeezed her eyes shut. It was like high school all over again. Except she hadn't been pregnant then, just the victim of a vicious rumor. Not that it had stopped her boyfriend from dumping her when word got out.

And if she could count on one thing, it was that Sebastian would not react well to her being pregnant. He would think she'd done it on purpose. All her talk of getting married and babies. He would believe she'd tricked him, and who could blame him? It's what his ex-wife had done.

But he'd marry her. And spend the rest of his life resenting her the way he resented his first wife. Missy couldn't bear that. She loved him too much to put him through it. So, she wouldn't tell him.

Her phone rang. It was a Houston number, but not Sebastian's.

"Missy," Max Case boomed. "I hope your father is doing better."

"Yes, much. Thank you." She stared at the stick and watched the blue bar coalesce.

Positive. Pregnant.

"Glad to hear it. Do you still want the director of communications position?"

She couldn't be pregnant. She didn't have a husband. No job meant no income, no health coverage. What was she going to do?

"I'm sorry, Max, you broke up." What had he said? "Could you say that again?"

"I asked if you're still interested in Dean's job."

This answered the problem of her job situation, but what about Sebastian? A second ago she'd decided that she wouldn't tell Sebastian he was going to be a father. Could she have his baby and stay working around him at the same time?

"Missy?" Max prompted. "Are you still there?"

"Yes."

"So, what do you say?"

What could she say? "I'm still interested in the job. I'm just worried about Sebastian's reaction."

"Don't let it stop you from what will be a wonderful career move."

"You're right. I'll take the job. And thank you."

"When are you coming back?"

She scrubbed her cheeks free of tears and shook her shoulders like a dog shedding water. With her spine as stiff as she could make it, she exited the bathroom and headed for the truck.

"I'll head home Wednesday," she said, wishing she could linger in Crusade and hide from her troubles a little longer.

"I'll see you in the office on Thursday."

"Max, can you let me tell Sebastian about the job?"

"If that's what you want."

"It is."

Missy sighed as she ended the call. Sebastian would be unhappy that she hadn't talked to him about staying on at Case Consolidated Holdings before accepting the job.

Hopefully he would be glad she was sticking around. From the start, he'd made it clear that his need for her started and stopped at the office. Besides, no matter how amazing the sex between them had been, they'd both known it was only a matter of time before Sebastian came to his senses and relegated what had happened between them in Vegas to a massive mistake.

Or perhaps he'd figured it out already. Although she heard from him almost every day, their conversations were strictly business. She couldn't help but wonder if Sebastian had been going out with Kaitlyn. His mother wanted him to marry the wealthy socialite. Missy understood why. They were a perfect social and economic match. Sebastian was practical. Was it only a matter of time until he saw the advantages?

Could she work at Case Consolidated Holdings and watch him marry someone else while she raised his child on her own? Missy grimaced. It would be hell. And she'd spent enough years pining after a man she couldn't have.

Lightning arced across the sky overhead. A storm had blown in while she'd awaited the results of the pregnancy test. By the time she got a mile down the road, rain hammered the truck roof like angry fists. Visibility diminished to ten feet in front of her. Driving in these conditions was beyond reckless. But she couldn't shake an urgent need to get home.

The windshield wipers flew back and forth at top speed, but as quickly as they cleared water from the windshield, more replaced it. A pair of lights appeared before her, too close for her to stop. She swerved toward the shoulder and hit the brakes. The tires caught in the soft gravel, turned to thick mud by the downpour and pulled the truck even farther from the road. Coming to a full stop, she gripped the wheel hard. A jackhammer pounded away in her chest.

The near miss had brought crystalline clarity. No matter what happened between her and Sebastian, this wasn't just about them anymore. She was going to be a mother. Maybe sooner than she'd expected and without hope that the father would ever believe she'd had no ulterior motive when she slept with him. But she had a new focus for her life. Going forward, every decision she made would be with her child's best interest as her priority.

And if that meant working as the director of communications for Case Consolidated Holdings and letting the love of her life never know he was the father of her child, that's what she'd do.

Nine

Sebastian raced home, hoping to beat Missy there. Her plane had landed an hour ago, but the heavy rush-hour traffic from the airport would probably double her half-hour commute. He checked his cell, expecting an irate phone call when she discovered the car he'd sent to fetch her wasn't taking her to her house but to his.

Being separated from her for a month had taken its toll on him both professionally and personally. He'd gone through three temps, the longest one lasting nine business days before dissolving into tears.

"Impossible to find good help," he muttered, turning into his driveway, his fingers tapping an impatient rhythm on the armrest as the wrought iron gates swung open.

The neighborhood where he'd built was an eclectic mix—mid-century ranches and twenty-first-century mansions. Close to downtown Houston and boasting a highly desirable school system, many people, himself included, had bought an older home on a large lot with mature trees and torn down the house to make way for a mini estate.

A black town car idled near the front door. He parked

behind the vehicle and got out. As he approached the car, he driver met him by the rear passenger door.

"Good afternoon, Mr. Case."

"Hello, Burt." Sebastian used this driver often when he raveled. "Did Miss Ward go inside?"

"No, sir," the driver said, hand on the door handle. "She wanted to wait until you got home."

"How long have you been here?"

"Ten minutes." He opened the door.

Sebastian peered in, expecting to catch the brunt of Missy's annoyance and found her curled sideways on the seat, cheek cradled on her hand, asleep. The sight dismantled all he walls he'd erected around his emotions. In an instant he was transported back to their first night together when he'd spent an hour watching her sleep.

Crouching beside the car, he skimmed a russet strand of her hair behind her ear. When she didn't stir, he scooped her into his arms. "Bring her bag," he told the driver as he strode up his front steps.

His housekeeper must have been watching from the window because the door opened as he neared it. Without pausing, he carried Missy up the wide marble stairs and down the hallway to his bedroom.

How taxing had her time away from him been that she'd fallen asleep in ten short minutes? Hadn't her brothers and their wives pitched in? Or had everyone taken advantage of her generous nature and let Missy shoulder all the nursing duty?

She woke as he eased her down onto the mattress. "Sebastian?" She reached up and touched his cheek, her eyes soft and barely focused.

"I missed you," he admitted, stretching out beside her.

She rolled onto her side and snuggled against him. "Missed you, too," she murmured into his neck, her warm breath puffing against him. Her fingers tunneled beneath his tie and between his shirt buttons, finding skin.

Instantly aroused, he cupped the side of her face in his palm and brought his mouth to hers. Desire blindsided him. Going without her in his arms for a month had turned him into a ravenous bear. He feasted off her soft sighs and the press of her lithe body against his. Rolling with her across his king-size bed, he stripped her down to her underwear and settled between her thighs, his jacket, tie and shoes gone, his shirt ripped open by her impatience.

Breathing in her delicious scent, he drifted his lips down her throat and between her breasts to the lacy edge of her bra. Drawing his tongue along the edge of the lace, he savored the rapid rise and fall of her chest as his fingers tickled up her thigh.

"Make love to me," she gasped, her fingers coasting down his sides and burrowing between their bodies in search of his belt. "I need to feel you inside me."

Her words inflamed his already overstimulated body. "Don't rush me. I intend to get reacquainted with every inch of you before that happens."

"I can't wait that long." She rotated her hips, bringing his erection into better contact with her core.

Even through the layers that separated them, he could feel how she burned for him. That knowledge pushed him over the edge. In seconds he'd shed the rest of his clothes and come back to find her naked and waiting for him.

Driving into her tight sheath, he groaned as she closed around him, drawing him deeper inside. He buried his face in her neck. Her fingernails sank into his back as they moved together, as connected in soul as they were joined in body.

He struggled to hold off his climax, but her impassioned cries and urgent movements slashed the tethers binding his willpower. Reaching between their bodies, he touched her setting off the chain reaction of her orgasm. With a final thrust he let out a triumphant cry.

"That wasn't the homecoming I pictured," he muttered, rolling over so her limp body draped across his chest like an erotic daydream.

She nuzzled his neck. "Really? It's all I thought about."

Her round backside called to his hand. He followed the curve with his fingers, measuring the perfect rise from the small of her back to her thigh. Every inch of her fascinated him. Contentment settled over him as he stroked her hip with his thumb.

She raised her head and braced her forearm against his chest. Her voice may have been light and airy a second ago, but she wore a serious expression now.

"Something on your mind?" he prompted as the silence stretched.

"I'm just going to come right out and say this."

But still she struggled with whatever she needed to tell him. Making love to her had pacified his earlier impatience. He kept silent and let her work out whatever was bothering her.

"I think it would be better if we got dressed first."

She shimmied off his body, her long hair falling forward to conceal her expression as she retrieved her clothes and slid into jeans and shirt. Jerky movements and her lack of playfulness warned him something serious was up with her. He ignored the agitation that flared in his gut. The month-long separation had been harder on him than expected. Now that she was within his grasp once more he wanted nothing disagreeable to distract him from the pleasure of watching her.

She tossed his boxers at him. As he slipped them over his hips, the words erupted from her.

"Tomorrow I'm starting as the new director of communications."

* * *

If the situation were reversed, and Sebastian had kept something this big from her, Missy would have stormed hard enough to level a house.

But Missy never knew him to thunder and rage like a summer squall. No, Sebastian had a calm, icy way of being furious that was ten times worse.

"When did this happen?" There was enough frost in his voice to ruin an entire orange crop.

"Your father mentioned the idea to me in Las Vegas." She searched his rigid expression, assessing just how angry he was. "Then Max called me a few days ago and I said yes."

"I see."

What did he see? That she was perfect for the job? That discussing a job with his father and brother made her feel disloyal and low? That she loved him so much she'd rather spend every day thirty feet down the hall than never see him again?

"Are you okay with it?"

"We can't keep seeing each other if you work for Case Consolidated Holdings."

"I considered that." Was it wrong of her to choose something sensible like a fabulous job instead of a risky venture like dating Sebastian for as long as he wanted her? The old her, the impulsive girl who'd made a brief appearance in Las Vegas, would have chosen an uncertain future with Sebastian. Unfortunately, she'd spent more than a decade making decisions with her head, not her heart. "But we'd already agreed that once we left Las Vegas it was over between us."

"That's what you wanted. I had something different in mind."

She refused to feel guilty for disappointing him. It was ridiculous to think she could keep his interest long-term. "I'm perfect for this job."

"Then if the job is what you want, you should take it."

Throat too tight for words to escape, Missy nodded. Sebastian's impassive acceptance of her decision left her stomach in knots. But what had she expected? An impassioned plea for her to choose him over her career? Eventually he'd be glad she'd given him the perfect out.

Wrung out and miserable, she let Sebastian take on the bulk of the conversational duties as he drove her home. He asked her about her family and updated her on what had happened with the business since she'd been gone. By unspoken consent, they avoided discussing the elephants crowded in the backseat: her new job, how everyone at the office would react to her promotion and what had happened between them an hour earlier.

"Thank you for sending the car to pick me up," she said as he carried her suitcase into the condo she rented. Feeling awkward for the first time ever around him, she fiddled with her purse strap and wondered if she should offer him something to drink.

"You're welcome." He bent down and grazed his lips against hers.

Although the touch of Sebastian's kisses would forever cause her to melt like snow in the tropics, Missy's stomach clenched in despair. The brief kiss was goodbye.

"I'll see you tomorrow morning," she said.

"I have a breakfast meeting. I'll stop by your new office when I get in."

He left her standing in the middle of her living room, nodding after him like a bobble-head doll. He'd changed from ardent lover to supportive ex-boss so fast she had whiplash. She was glad she'd decided against telling him about the baby.

Once her pregnancy became public knowledge, she'd let everyone believe Tim was the father. No reason to let what had happened between her and Sebastian in Vegas create life-long consequences for him. So what if her instincts told her what she was doing was wrong? She'd ignored her gut feelings for fifteen years and let her head lead. She'd grown accustomed to weighing options. Logic dictated her actions.

Back when she'd been a teenager, she'd learned what happened if she let her heart run amuck.

Pity she hadn't remembered those lessons in Vegas.

Sebastian let himself into his parents' house. He was furious with his father for interfering in the running of the business again and angry with himself for not thinking of putting Missy into the communications director position himself.

"Sebastian," his mother said, getting up from the computer in her office. "What are you doing here?"

"I came to talk to Dad."

She surveyed his expression. "What did he do now?"

"He offered Missy a job without telling me."

"I'm sure he had good intentions."

"You give him the benefit of the doubt too often." Sebastian tempered his tone. After all, he wasn't angry with his mother. "Where is he?"

Following his mother's directions, Sebastian found his father in the library. "You offered Missy the communications director job?"

"Hello, Sebastian." Brandon pulled off his reading glasses. "I did."

"Why did you do that?"

"Because she belongs with us. And she can do the job. You should've promoted her years ago. If you had, maybe she wouldn't have quit."

Sebastian bit back a growl. As much as he hated to admit it, his father was right. Missy was overqualified to be his assistant. He'd been a selfish bastard to keep her as long as he had.

"You should have talked to me first."

"I spoke with Max. She'd be working for him. He liked the idea."

How could Sebastian argue? His father's logic was flawless. It was his methods that set Sebastian to grinding his teeth. Nor would he stop Missy from taking a job she so obviously wanted more than she wanted to keep seeing him.

He wasn't about to admit he'd realized he was glad she'd resigned. That he was glad she'd be sleeping in his bed instead of working for his company. Letting passion dominate reason went against everything he believed in. So, why did he want to hit something?

"Why didn't anyone talk to me about it?"

"Missy wanted to be the one to break the news."

"I wish you'd come to me before speaking to Missy. I would have liked the opportunity to offer her the position."

"Sorry we left you out of the loop." Brandon didn't look one bit sorry that he'd bypassed Sebastian and asserted his authority once again. "After I found out she'd quit, the decision happened pretty fast. I spoke to her about it in Las Vegas, but because of what happened to her dad, she didn't give us her answer until a couple days ago."

She'd kept this from him for a month.

"You've been busy with Smythe Industries," her father continued. "I don't see why you're so annoyed. We're keeping a valuable employee."

And Sebastian had lost the ability to pursue a personal relationship with her.

The temptation to ask his father to back off held Sebastian mute. He'd never felt less like a leader in his life. Leaders were the ones with all the answers. The ones in control. He was neither.

"Missy will make a terrific communications director," his father said. "You'll see."

Sebastian offered his father a tight smile. "I don't doubt that for a second."

"Then this isn't about me interfering?"

"Do you want to be CEO again?" Sebastian wasn't sure

where the question came from. He only knew he was ready to walk away from the job he was born to do. Maybe he'd go work for a Fortune 500 corporation. Or start his own company. Do something that wouldn't involve family. "Say the word and I'm gone."

From the surprise on his father's face, Sebastian could see he was finally getting through.

"I don't want to run the company. Retirement…"

"Is boring as hell. I get it. Mom wanted me to convince you to stay retired. She's enjoying having you around. Heaven knows why when all you do is golf." Sebastian set his hands on his hips. "I think she's scared if you go back to work it will aggravate your heart problems. But maybe she's wrong to keep you from something you love so much."

"Sebastian?" His mother entered the room. How much had she heard? "Can you stay for dinner?"

"No. I'm heading back to the office. Without Missy's help these past few weeks, I'm behind." He shot his father one last look. "You were right to want her to stay with the company. I just hope you did it for the right reasons."

Sebastian eased his car toward the curb in front of the downtown Houston hotel. As he put it into Park, a valet stepped up to the passenger door. Missy smoothed her hands down the front of her cornflower-blue cocktail dress. The gown's silky material grazed her curves with elegant style. The cool color contrasted wonderfully with her red hair.

"I don't see why you needed me to come here with you," she complained, questioning his motives for about the tenth time. Her tension was palpable in the confined space. She'd been clenching her evening bag hard the entire drive from her house.

"Because you're our director of communications and there are a lot of people attending that you should meet." For the past two weeks, he'd been keeping discreet tabs on her.

She stepped into a position without anyone to show her the ropes. That couldn't have been easy. Sebastian knew no one who could have handled the transition as well as Missy had. "Relax." He took her hand, compelled by a strong need to reassure her.

"Easy for you to say—you do this all the time."

"There's nothing to it." He stepped out of the car and circled the vehicle. "Just picture them all in their underwear."

For a second his suggestion flustered her. She stared at him in astonishment before a wry grin curved her lips. "I thought that only worked for public speaking," she said, tucking her purse into the crook of her arm and letting him guide her into the elegant lobby.

"It works anytime you need it."

The organizers of the fundraising event—which was geared toward supporting a local food shelf—had decided a casino night was a fun and profitable way to raise funds. Sebastian experienced a moment of déjà vu as they entered the ballroom.

Missy rubbed her hands together gleefully, her earlier nerves forgotten. "Time to take a little cash home."

"This is a charity event," Sebastian murmured, amused by the frankness of her avarice. "I think the idea is to leave your cash on the table."

"How about I try not to win as much as you lose?"

Sebastian gripped her elbow and steered her toward the roulette table. "What makes you think you're going to win?"

"You're my good luck charm, aren't you?" A flirtatious glance slipped from beneath her eyelashes.

"Is that all I am to you?"

Before she could answer, a man stepped into their path. With a drink in his left hand and an ingratiating smile plastered on his face, he swung his palm toward Sebastian. An executive in name only at one of Houston's larger banks, Bob Stokes attended these functions because his wealthy wife liked being seen with her attractive younger husband as much as she enjoyed flaunting her family's money.

"Good to see you again, Sebastian."

"Bob." He gave a curt nod as he crushed the man's hand in a firm handshake. "This is Missy Ward," he added. "Bob Stokes."

Missy murmured a polite greeting that was scarcely acknowledged by the man. Her gaze shifted past the interruption toward the roulette table. Sebastian felt her sigh as Bob launched into a detailed description of his new driver and how it had improved his golf game.

"Sorry, I don't golf," Sebastian said, turning down an invitation to join the man at his club. "If you want to talk about drivers, catch up with my father. He's the enthusiast."

"You don't golf?"

Sebastian was too busy running a multimillion-dollar corporation to putter around on the links like so many of his colleagues. He'd always believed that the boss should work harder than any of his employees. His father had never shared that opinion. Brandon had only worked as hard as he had to. That partially explained why the company's profits had been so erratic during his father's stewardship.

Steering Missy around Bob, they resumed their trek toward the roulette wheel. Five steps later, he was waylaid again.

"You came," the petite brunette exclaimed. Ignoring Missy completely, she rose on tiptoe and kissed Sebastian on both cheeks. "Wait until I tell Gina that Sebastian Case came to my fundraiser. Stay here while I fetch her."

"We're heading for the roulette table," Sebastian told her.

"We?" The brunette blinked her bright-blue eyes in confusion.

Sebastian turned to Missy. "Missy Ward. Communications director for Case Consolidated Holdings. Tanya Hart."

The brunette frowned at Missy as if trying to place her.

"Nice to meet you." Suddenly she began waving to someone across the room. "Don't move," she commanded.

As Tanya sped off into the crowd, Missy said, "Remind me again why I'm here."

"You need to meet the movers and shakers in this town."

"Well, apparently, they're not terribly interested in meeting me."

From her mild tone, she sounded unaffected by the brushoffs she'd received, but the corners of her lips tightened, betraying her misery.

"They will be." He gave the words a fierce punch. "Let's go lose some money."

A bright smile emerged. "You mean win some money, don't you?"

Sebastian avoided eye contact with everyone as they approached the tables set up for gambling and focused his entire attention on Missy. How had he not anticipated this evening might be uncomfortable for her? Maybe because he'd seized the opportunity to spend some time away from the office with her. Maybe because he'd never seen these people through someone else's eyes.

He bought five thousand dollars' worth of chips and nudged the stack directly in front of Missy. "Time to see if your luck is still holding," he told her.

As eager as she'd been to play five minutes earlier, she now backed away from the table.

"That's a lot of money," she said, her gaze fixed on the pile of chips.

"It's no more than you gambled in Vegas on a single turn of the wheel."

"That was different."

"How exactly?" He leaned his hand on the table so he could peer at her expression.

"That was my money."

"Think of it as a donation to charity." He pushed five one

hundred dollar chips onto black. "Care to make a side bet with me?"

She nudged a single chip onto the red, her gaze flicking toward him with interest. "What did you have in mind?"

"If I win, you spend the night at my house."

The ball began its circuit of the wheel. Missy didn't seem to breathe as the circling silver blur slowed.

"We can't do that. I'm your employee, remember?"

Sebastian lowered his lips within an inch of her ear. "I miss you."

Even though they weren't touching, he felt tension exit her muscles.

"I miss you, too," she whispered. "But if it lands on red, you don't ask me again."

"Double zero," the dealer called.

They'd both lost.

Missy began to laugh. "Maybe that's fate's way of telling us we should leave well enough alone."

Sebastian didn't care for the sound of that. Not one bit.

Ten

Between Missy's good luck and Sebastian's bad, the height of the chip pile remained constant until a man in his mid-fifties approached, keen on getting Sebastian's opinion on the current political climate in Austin. The conversation held no interest for Missy so she excused herself and headed for the ladies' room.

When she emerged from the bathroom stall, a brunette with long silky hair stood at the sinks, reapplying her lipstick. Missy felt the woman's gaze on her as she washed her hands.

"Are you Sebastian's date?" the woman asked.

"No. Heavens, no." Missy's laugh sounded hysterical to her ears. "I'm the director of communications for Case Consolidated Holdings."

"Oh." The woman's sunny smile could have cut through the thickest fog. "I'm Kaitlyn Murray."

The woman Sebastian had been seeing casually for six months before the Vegas trip. The one his mother thought Sebastian should propose to.

"Nice to meet you. We've spoken on the phone. I'm Missy Ward, Sebastian's former assistant."

"You've been out for a while. Sebastian said your father had been in an accident."

Okay, so Kaitlyn was genuinely nice, a delightful change from the other people she'd met that evening. And she and Sebastian had been in contact since he'd returned from Las Vegas. Missy wasn't surprised.

"If you call being stabbed an accident, then yes."

"Stabbed?" Kaitlyn looked shocked. Undoubtedly she couldn't fathom that sort of violence entering her gilded world. "How awful. What happened?"

"My father's a minister. He went to the aid of one of his parishioners and got between her and the boyfriend who was trying to hurt her. He's fine now," Missy assured her, seeing that her bald summary of the facts had shaken the woman. "The guy's in jail."

"I should hope so." Kaitlyn dropped her lipstick into her clutch. "Are you enjoying yourself tonight?"

"I'm afraid I'm a little out of my element."

"Oh? Why is that?"

"I'm from a small town in west Texas. Events like this are so intimidating. Half the time I have no idea what people are talking about."

A mischievous smile broke out on Kaitlyn's beautiful face. "I'll give you a little insider's tip. Most of the time they don't know what they're talking about, either."

As Missy laughed, some of her insecurities faded. She really liked Kaitlyn. No wonder Susan hoped her son would ask the socialite to marry him. "How long have you and Sebastian known each other?"

"Oh, forever. My daddy and his went to college together and remain the best of friends. I practically grew up with Sebastian, Max and Nathan. Of course, I'm a lot younger than them. They treated me like a pesky little sister."

"I know that feeling exactly," she said, liking the woman more and more even as her heart grew heavy at how perfectly

Kaitlyn fit into Sebastian's world. Same background. Same lifestyle. "I have four older brothers that I used to tag after like a lost puppy."

"Exactly." Kaitlyn's laugh rolled from her throat in a melodious ripple. "I thought one day they might see me as something else." She shrugged. "But all any of us will ever be is friends. It was nice to meet you."

"Nice meeting you," Missy echoed.

She lingered in the bathroom, powdering her nose and applying lipstick. Meeting Kaitlyn had put her in a thoughtful mood. Ever since high school, she'd envied the girls like her. They all navigated this world of wealth and sophistication with such ease. She felt gauche and awkward beside them. If she and Kaitlyn stood on either side of Sebastian, onlookers would always assume he and Kaitlyn were the couple. They both exuded a confidence that Missy couldn't match.

All the more reason to stick to her plan and keep things strictly professional between them. With a grimace, Missy exited the restroom and searched for Sebastian.

"I've gambled away all the money," he said as she approached. "Let's get out of here."

"But we've only been here an hour." Was he already embarrassed that she didn't fit in with his crowd?

He looked displeased with her answer. "I suppose you want the chance to win the money back." He slid his fingers over the small of her back and applied the perfect pressure to coax her closer. "I've made an appearance and done my duty by the food shelf. Now, I want to take you home."

That's what she was afraid of. "Sure. Tomorrow's a work-day after all. I suppose we should make it an early night."

"You misunderstand me," Sebastian said, his eyes alight. Her pulse skyrocketed as the compelling warmth of his hand penetrated her silk dress. "Will you be angry if I tell you tonight was merely an excuse to spend time with you?"

Her mouth dropped open as his meaning penetrated, but

already her longing for him was threatening her common sense. "You're making a huge mistake."

"I don't follow."

She gestured at her hair and clothes. "This isn't me. Las Vegas was nothing but a fantasy."

"I think this is you."

"No. I'm the girl who works long hours at a job she's over-qualified for and spends her free time knitting prayer shawls and volunteering at women-at-risk shelters. I don't drink. I don't club. I'm not glamorous or interesting." She kept her face turned away so he couldn't see the hot tears brimming in her eyes.

"Have you looked in the mirror? You're beautiful. And the most fascinating woman in the world." His compliments might be a complete lie, but they weakened her knees all the same. "Now, let's get out of here."

After that speech, how could she be anything but putty in his hands? Fortunately, their exit was delayed by a half-dozen more people who asked about business, or mentioned his father or tried to corral him for lunch. She recognized a majority of the men. Many she'd spoken with on the phone during her four years working for Sebastian.

They, in turn, seemed surprised to see her at Sebastian's side during a nonwork event. She could almost hear them wonder why Sebastian brought his former executive assistant to the fundraiser. Despite being introduced as the new director of communications, she couldn't stop feeling like an outsider.

If it were only Sebastian and her, she wouldn't have a care in the world. His kisses banished every worry from her mind like magic. Every time they came together it was a roller-coaster ride of desire. But real relationships existed in public as well as private. She couldn't picture herself ever fitting into his world.

On the way back to her condo, Sebastian drove in silence.

His fingers tapped the steering wheel, keeping time to a rhythm only he heard. Almost as if he was anxious. Unaccustomed to anything but utter calm from him, she eyed Sebastian from beneath her lashes.

"I met Kaitlyn Murray at the party," she said. "She seems very nice."

"Kaitlyn is a great girl."

"She said your families are very close."

"I guess that's true." Sebastian shot her a questioning look.

"Your mom's right. She's the perfect choice for you. She knows all the same people you do. Attends the same events. I'm sure she went to all the right schools."

"And I feel nothing but friendship toward her."

"You could build on that."

"It might have been enough once." Sebastian let his gaze slide over her. "Before I got to know you in Las Vegas."

Her heart felt lighter than air. For a second it was hard to breathe. Before she floated away, Missy got herself back under control. Nothing about their situation had changed. "What happened between us there was just passion."

"Then why can't I stop thinking about you?"

His words awakened a tremor. "It just didn't get a chance to burn out."

"That's your explanation?" Sebastian nodded. "If we'd been together for a couple months, maybe a year I'd have gotten tired of you. Is that what you think?"

"Something like that. Only it might not have taken longer than a couple weeks. I don't fit in your world. Tonight proved it."

"Proved it how? Do you seriously think a bunch of blowhards are my world? Or those two-dimensional women whose lives revolve around parties and spending money?" Sebastian's voice softened. "What the hell made you such a cynic?"

Missy hesitated. It wasn't her proudest moment, but if he

knew the truth, he might realize why they'd never work outside the bedroom.

"When I was a sophomore in high school I dated a guy from the wealthiest family in the county. He was a senior and heading to college on a football scholarship. We'd talk for hours about the future. He couldn't wait to get out of Crusade. His daddy owned the bank. Chip was supposed to get a business degree and come back."

"Chip?" Sebastian repeated the name.

"Robert. His daddy called him a chip off the old block and the name stuck." She always smiled when she remembered those months before her world crumbled. "But Chip's dreams were bigger than Crusade and that's what I loved about him. Not his fancy car like my family thought or his money. He was going to reach for the stars and I wanted to be right beside him, living my own dreams."

Her voice faded. Funny how fifteen years later her dreams consisted of spending two years saving for a fairytale wedding gown, only to have her boyfriend dump her in favor of a woman he scarcely knew.

"So, you dated a rich kid with big dreams. What happened?"

"His friends never liked that I was dating him. They thought being with me lowered his status. One of them started a rumor that I'd gotten pregnant on purpose hoping that he'd marry me."

Why even now did her mouth go dry when she remembered how he'd screamed at her, calling her a stupid slut who'd ruined his life? It was fifteen years in the past, yet as vivid as if it had happened yesterday.

"Maybe I believed myself in love with him. And, sure, I considered what being married to him would be like—but I wasn't trying to get pregnant. I was on the pill and I made him use protection. But he freaked out. Dumped me. Ruined my reputation." She eased her death grip on her clutch. Forced her shoulders to relax. "Told everyone I'd done lots of things." The rest of the explanation wouldn't come. Sebastian would just have to use his imagination. "Needless to say, my family was horrified. My mom had suffered a stroke a couple months before. Dad grounded me for about a year. Which was okay. My social life was over."

"I'm sorry you had to go through that. But the party tonight wasn't high school."

"No. But the concept is the same. Chip dumped me because his friends believed I wasn't good enough for him and made him believe terrible things about me. Those were your friends in there tonight."

"Not my friends. Business associates and acquaintances."

"But they're your social circle. They didn't welcome me with open arms."

"You're comparing me to some weak-minded boy. Do you really imagine I would turn on you like that?"

"I never said you would." But it wasn't only about the two of them. She was pregnant. What if he wanted to marry her? She'd eventually disappoint him. Or worse, he'd be too furious to ever want to see her again. "But you can't blame a girl for wanting to protect herself from getting hurt."

After leaving Missy at her front door with a kiss designed to get him inside her apartment—a kiss that failed—Sebastian swung by Nathan and Emma's. His new sister-in-law crafted jewelry. Dazzling one-of-a-kind pieces that had garnered her some great publicity and made demand for her work soar.

That's why, with a minor difficulty with her pregnancy slowing her down and the demand for her work increasing, Sebastian had to wait three weeks for the special piece he'd commissioned.

Nathan answered Sebastian's knock, looking none too pleased at his brother's late appearance. Already dressed for bed, he blocked Sebastian's entrance with his hand on the door. "You're the mystery client she's been working night and day for?"

"Hardly night and day," Emma said, ducking under her husband's arm. She smiled at Sebastian. "He worries too much."

"You heard the doctor. You're supposed to take it easy."

"It's a little high blood pressure."

"It's preeclampsia." Nathan's tone made it sound like a death sentence.

"Forgive my husband," Emma said. "Come in. Your order is ready."

"Order?" Nathan echoed, stepping back as his wife applied an elbow to his ribs. He trailed her as far as the living room. When she headed into her workroom, he rounded on Sebastian. "What sort of order did you place with my wife that has kept her up late working?"

Sebastian observed the changes in his sibling with interest. Nathan had such a casual, freewheeling style at work. Nothing much seemed to bother him. He handled successes and setbacks with the same cool confidence.

His pregnant wife, however, brought out a keen, possessive side.

"It's nothing I feel like talking about at the moment."

"You're keeping her from getting the rest she needs. I think I have the right to know why."

"I'm sorry if I've caused problems. It wasn't my intention to put her health at risk."

"You didn't." Emma returned and nudged her husband with her hip.

Nathan's hand settled on her round belly. "You've barely rested all week."

"I'm pregnant," she said, covering his hand with hers. "Not an invalid."

"What did you make for him?"

"Sebastian asked me not to say anything to anyone." She

handed Sebastian a box and wrapped her arms around her husband's waist.

Nathan visibly relaxed in his wife's embrace. "I'm your husband. You should be able to tell me everything."

"Nice try." She reached up on tiptoe and kissed his chin. "Would you make me a snack while I walk Sebastian out? I bought some fresh strawberries today."

"We're out of whipped cream."

"But there's chocolate sauce." Her eyes took on a particular softness as she gazed up at her husband.

"Fine." Grumbling, Nathan headed deeper into the condo.

Watching Nathan and Emma awakened Sebastian to envy. After his disastrous first marriage, he'd refused to let emotion lead him back to the altar. He'd approached his personal relationships more like business deals, analyzing, weighing the pros and cons of each potential merger.

Until that night in Las Vegas with Missy.

Missy was real and endlessly fascinating. He adored her ability to sit back and observe and then arrow straight to the heart of someone's character. How many times had he brought her into his office and wrestled an opinion out of her when a problem came up in one of their divisions?

She dismantled his restraint with her audacious opinions of him and her enthusiasm for adventure. His desire for her astonished him, but he could no more fight it than stop an avalanche.

Tonight, what he'd learned of her past left him with concerns. She'd obviously suffered at the hands of a teenage idiot with no thought of anyone but himself, but how badly damaged was her ability to trust? She claimed she didn't view him in the same light as her high school boyfriend, but Sebastian wondered if she intended to hold his wealth and position against him.

He'd thought a lot about Missy during the four weeks she'd been gone. And that had led to missing her. He'd invented excuses to call her once, even twice, a day, just so he could hear her voice.

The behavior struck him as unnecessary, yet he couldn't stop himself from dialing. He hated that she was on his mind all day long. He wasn't in control of his actions or his thoughts, and fighting the need to connect with her a dozen times a day warned him he might be on the path to even more disastrous tendencies like skipping work to spend the day in bed with her or clearing his schedule so he could enjoy her company over a long lunch.

Her new job might have created a wall between them, but it was a flimsy barrier to Sebastian's desires. A more formidable impediment was convincing her to trust him to keep her safe in his social circles.

It was a task he was up to. Tonight had demonstrated how much he wanted her in his life.

"Sorry about my husband," Emma said with an apologetic shrug. "He's become a little unreasonable since our last doctor visit."

Sebastian was on the verge of telling his sister-in-law that her husband had a knack for being unreasonable when he realized that a certain woman had accused him of the exact same failing. Maybe all the Case men were cursed with a gene that made them more of a handful than the average man.

While Emma walked him to the front door, Sebastian cracked the lid on the box and stared at the contents. Diamonds shot sparks at him from their nest of black velvet.

"This is incredible," he told her. "The sketches don't do your work justice."

Emma sagged into her smile. "Thank you. With all the success I've had you'd think I'd get used to people liking my work. But this piece is special. It's going to sound silly but working on it felt magical."

"Not silly at all. You are a true artist." He leaned down and kissed his sister-in-law on the cheek. "Thanks, Emma. I hope my brother knows how lucky he is to have you."

"I know." Nathan stood just inside the foyer, arms crossed, eyes flashing with annoyance. "And as soon as you get the hell out of here, I'm going to give her a demonstration she won't soon forget."

Her new office as the director of communications gave Missy less square footage than the cubicle she'd had outside Sebastian's executive suite. But it had a door. And a window.

At the moment, she was enjoying both.

Sipping the tea she'd picked up on the way in, Missy watched as the building next door turned to gold in the dawn light. Why was she at work at six-thirty in the morning? Because yesterday she'd left early to go to a doctor's appointment and because she was worried about doing a good job in her new position.

A firm knock on her door warned her she had company. Only one man got to the office this early.

"Good morning, Missy." Sebastian surveyed her with a toe-curling grin. "You're in awfully early."

For the past three days, he'd made an effort to pop by and say hello. In all the years she'd worked for him, she'd never seen him so chipper. It was unnerving.

"I had some things to catch up on."

Shoulder propped against her doorframe, he eyed her cup. "You're drinking tea?" Commenting on her daily caffeine jumpstart was a typical morning conversation opener for him. "That's a change."

"I haven't been sleeping well so I'm cutting out caffeine." Her eyes burned.

She hadn't slept well since discovering she was pregnant. Too many worries crowded her. During the day she mastered anxiety by throwing herself into learning the ins and outs of her new job.

"What you need is some exercise before bedtime." He'd also taken to flirting with her. "I could help you with that."

"No." Heavens. That was the last thing she needed. "It's the new position. I have a lot to learn."

"You were always a perfectionist." He took a step into her office. "Max is very happy with what you're doing. So relax."

Some of her tension eased, but her dizziness remained. "Thanks, that's good to know."

"It's my mother's birthday on Friday. There's a family get-together at their house. Will you come?"

It wasn't an unusual request. She'd celebrated occasions with his family before. Nothing had changed except she no longer worked directly for him. Yet, her instincts told her to refuse.

"I'd like to, but it's Memorial Day weekend and I'm heading home to check on my father."

Not a complete fabrication. She'd told her family she'd try to make the annual Ward barbecue.

"She specifically asked me to invite you. She'll be very disappointed if you aren't there. My father has some big surprise planned. She's worried it could end up being a disaster."

Missy felt herself weakening. She really loved Susan. And Brandon had gone out of his way to make certain she took this job. "I guess it would be okay if I took off for Crusade early Saturday morning."

"Excellent. I'll pick you up around six. Dinner's at seven."

Dinner with his family might not be out of the ordinary, but having Sebastian pick her up was. "I can drive myself."

"No need." His tone told her she'd be wasting her breath by arguing. "See you Friday."

"Friday," she echoed, wondering what the hell she'd just gotten herself into.

About a dozen times in the two days that followed, Missy started an email to Sebastian or picked up the phone to tell him she'd changed her mind. Since she'd slept with him in Las Vegas, she was no longer his overworked executive assistant. Now she was an ex-lover. The dynamic between them had altered, trapping her between craving his affection and dreading disappointment.

As Friday night rolled around, nerves unsettled her stomach so she used chocolate ice cream to settle both. Maybe not the best choice for a queasy pregnant woman, but she'd taken the last of the crackers to nibble on at work.

When the doorbell rang, she set the unfinished ice cream on her nightstand and went to answer it. She smoothed her hands down her dress and told herself to calm down. It was just a routine dinner at the Cases'.

But instead of Sebastian, Tim stood outside her door, a large cardboard box in his hands. He seemed shorter than she remembered. His blond hair thinner. And that crooked front tooth she'd always thought gave him character made her long for Sebastian's perfect smile.

"Wow." His eyes widened. "You look incredible."

"Thanks." She'd put on one of the new outfits she'd bought in Las Vegas, hoping to see Sebastian's eyes light up with that special glow that told her he appreciated what she was wearing if only so he could have the pleasure of taking it off. "What are you doing here?"

"I mean it." Tim stared at her as if he'd never really seen her before. "You look hot."

She glanced at the clock. It was five minutes to six. She had to make Tim leave and fast. "It's just a dress."

"It's more than the dress. You look completely different. Like wow."

The old her would have been thrilled by his enthusiasm. Tim wasn't much for compliments. Most of the time, he'd given her the impression he could do better. And since she'd worried that he was right, she'd never complained.

"Why weren't you like this when we were together?"

She refused to give him credit for her transformation, although she'd still be plain old Missy if he hadn't dumped her. "What's in there?" She gestured at the box he held.

"It's some of the stuff you left at my place. One of those shawls you knit. One of those books you read."

"It's a biography on John Adams. I left it for you. It was very good. I thought you would like it."

"That's okay. You know I don't read much." He used the box like a battering ram as he made his way into her condo. "Can I come in?"

"This isn't a great time." Knowing she'd never win a shoving match with Tim, Missy reluctantly gave ground. Anxiety hummed as he moved to the center of the living room and looked around. "You really need to go."

He shot her an exasperated look. "It'll just take a second for me to grab my anime DVDs."

"They're where you left them."

They'd never spent much time at Tim's house. He had a black Lab with no manners that Missy couldn't stand being around. Being unable to spend the night meant their sex life was sporadic. In fact, she couldn't remember the last time they'd been together. Unlike with Sebastian, where she felt each second without him as if an eternity had passed.

Had she seriously considered marrying Tim?

He dropped the box on her couch and turned toward her. "I broke up with Candy."

That explained his visit. He'd come by because he was alone once more, and if there was anything Tim hated, it was flying solo.

"That's too bad. You two seemed perfect for each other." A trace of bitterness entered her voice. Being dumped still stung even if her heart was no longer vulnerable to him.

"So did I until she left me." Tim looked ready to lay the whole sob story on her.

Missy edged toward Tim's anime collection. Sebastian was

due to arrive any second. The sooner she got rid of Tim, the better.

"It was then I realized I should never have broken up with you." He'd gotten that right at least. Too bad for him it was too little and way too late.

"That's sweet of you to say, but now you really have to go. I'm expecting someone…"

"I was hoping we could get back together."

He'd crushed her dreams without mercy, and now he wanted her to take him back? She almost laughed.

"I can't."

"Why not?" He really thought she'd still be pining over him.

And maybe he was right to. She'd let him treat her as if she wasn't good enough for him.

"Because I'm not the girl you dumped. More has happened to me in the last six weeks than new clothes and a better haircut." For one thing she was pregnant. For another, she'd fallen in love with the baby's father. Missy gathered a shaky breath as the hopelessness of her situation battered her. "I'm in love with someone else."

"In six weeks?" Tim scoffed, his eyes and mouth hardening. "That's not like you. It took a dozen dates before you'd let me kiss you. Is this your way of getting back at me?"

"No. It's true."

"Who is it?"

Missy hesitated. Tim had no right to any answer. It was none of his business.

"You're making this up," Tim cried, misinterpreting her pause. He grabbed her arms and pulled her close to his body. "You still love me. How could you not? We were together for three years. We talked about getting married."

Alarmed by her sudden predicament, she braced her hands on Tim's chest and pushed. Yes, they'd talked about it, but that's all they'd done. He hadn't proposed. Three years she waited for him, and he'd fallen in love with someone else and left her.

"Am I interrupting something?" A voice spoke from the front door.

Tim looked toward Sebastian and his expression darkened. He let her go. Missy stumbled back and caught herself on the rocking chair her grandfather had carved for her grandmother.

"I see the score now," Tim snarled. "He's what you want. He's all you ever wanted." Grabbing the videos he'd come for, Tim headed for the front door. He tried to muscle Sebastian out of the way and ended up bouncing off him like a pinball. "She's all yours. Not that it was ever in doubt."

Missy watched him go, her heart hammering at the expression on Sebastian's face. He didn't look overjoyed to find her in Tim's arms. Not that she'd been participating in the embrace.

"Was that your boyfriend?" His tone was neither conversational nor friendly.

"My ex-boyfriend."

"He didn't look very ex to me."

"He left me for his soul mate." She tried to keep the hurt from her voice. She didn't succeed. "I guess it didn't work out between them."

"And now he wants you back." Not a question, a statement. Sebastian's flat expression gave away none of his thoughts on the subject, but in his gray eyes, storm clouds gathered.

"He doesn't know what he wants."

"What about what you want?"

She was completely sure that she wanted Sebastian. He stirred her like no other man. The thought of waking up every morning to his handsome face made her blissful beyond words. But none of that changed the fact that she didn't fit into his world and never would.

When she didn't answer his question, Sebastian prowled toward her. "What do you want, Missy?"

"Nothing." She couldn't tell him the truth.

Sebastian captured her face in his hands, compelling her to meet his gaze. "Do you want him back? Because if you do, I'll chase him down."

"You would?" Missy regarded him in confusion. "Really?"

"No." His voice smiled, but his expression remained tense and watchful. "Maybe you need me to give you some help."

Her knees wobbled. "What sort of help?"

"I could tell you what I want."

"You've been pretty clear about that," she retorted dryly, but her banter didn't rouse a smile.

"No, I don't think I have. I want you. In my life. For as long as you'll have me."

Her breath caught.

She marveled at how his eyes glowed in the seconds before he captured her lips in the softest kiss imaginable. She remembered how his lovemaking had helped her overcome her fear of heights. Maybe it could help her overcome her fear of not fitting into his world.

"I'd like that, too," she breathed when he let her come up for air.

And between one exhalation and a gasp, he'd swung her off her feet and moved toward her bedroom.

"Wait. What about your mother's birthday party?"

"We'll be late."

He set her on her feet beside her bed, reached around her and grasped her zipper. His lips coasted along her neck as the dress came undone. Missy smiled, dazzled by the realization that she'd admitted her feelings to Sebastian and the sky hadn't fallen.

She was getting ready to shimmy out of her dress when Sebastian stilled all movement.

"How long after you two broke up did we make love?"

Every cell in her body froze solid. "A day." Lightheaded

with dismay, she nevertheless forced herself to ask, "Where are you going with this?"

He grabbed her upper arms and turned her toward her nightstand. Her throat trapped a small cry as she spied the pregnancy book she'd been reading before bed the previous night.

"Are you pregnant?"

"Yes."

"Were you planning on telling me?"

Misery engulfed her. "Yes." But she'd hesitated too long before answering.

His body vibrated with suppressed fury. "You set me up from the beginning, didn't you?"

"What?" She flinched away from the suspicion in his eyes. "No."

But he didn't hear her denial. Or if he had, he didn't believe her. His fingers bit into her flesh, keeping her pinned beneath his merciless stare.

"You found out you were pregnant. Your boyfriend dumped you. You seduced me so I'd believe the baby was mine."

His accusation came at her like a tire iron. Missy was too stunned to protect herself. Reeling from the impact, she struggled to breathe.

She wasn't surprised he'd jumped to that conclusion. His first wife had used a pregnancy lie to first get and then stay married to Sebastian. Why would he trust any woman after what he'd been through?

But that he believed it of her aligned all her defensives against him. She stiffened her muscles and straightened her spine. Digging the heel of her palms into his chest, she gave him back glare for glare.

But beneath her outrage, her heart had been gutted. The pain made trying to be strong so much harder. She thought she'd be better prepared for this moment. Hadn't she seen it coming the first morning after they'd made love? But knowing he'd eventually reject her and the reality of the experience were vastly different.

And deep down, she'd wanted to trust him. She'd even started to. After the casino night fundraiser, a seed of hope had sprouted. She'd fought to keep it from taking root, but with every fiber of her being she'd wanted things to work out between them. He'd sure done a good job convincing her she'd fit into his world. That he'd be by her side, protecting her.

Look how long that had lasted.

"Answer me, damn you," he ground out, looking ready to shake her unless she spilled everything. "Is the baby your boyfriend's?"

The lie she'd promised she'd tell him hovered on her tongue. It would be so easy to claim the baby was Tim's because it was clear that's what he was expecting to hear. She'd lose him. But isn't that what she'd decided was best for all concerned?

She lifted her arm and broke his hold. "This baby is mine. And no one else's."

"Stop evading the truth." He expelled the words through tight lips. His eyes blazed with fury and despair. "Who's the father?"

"What's the point in telling you? You're already convinced it's Tim's." Her head spun. At the moment, the only thing keeping her upright was her stubborn pride. "You need to go."

By some miracle she kept her voice steady. Telling herself this was for the best didn't make the loathing in Sebastian's gaze any easier to stomach. Tears burned the back of her eyes. She couldn't cry. She wouldn't.

Sebastian gathered in an enormous amount of air. His chest swelled with it. The condo was so silent Missy could hear the hum of the refrigerator in the kitchen. Her heart thumped in her ears. At last, he released his breath. His next words shocked her to her toes.

"I'm not going anywhere without you," he intoned. He'd

regained control of his emotions. "My family is waiting for us at my parents' house. We're supposed to be celebrating my mother's birthday."

"Your family is waiting for you." Faint with confusion, Missy shook her head. "I'm not going."

Why would he want to have anything to do with her after what they'd just been through? The answer jumped into her mind a second later. For the same reason he'd stayed married to Chandra despite all her craziness. He was a man who honored his commitments.

"You're going if I have to carry you out to my car."

Convinced he would act on his threat, she picked up her abandoned bowl of melted ice cream and dumped it over her head. She bit her lip to hold back a yelp as the sticky, cold liquid drenched her head and trickled beneath the neckline of her dress. She'd ruined her beautiful new dress, but the shock on Sebastian's face almost made up for the loss.

"Have you lost your mind?" he demanded.

"I lost it four years ago when I came to work for you." A hysterical giggle bubbled up, quickly followed by a ragged sob. Only Sebastian brought out such crazy impulses. The years she'd spent tempering her wild nature might never have been for all the control she exhibited around him.

"Go shower and change, I'll call and let everyone know we're going to be late."

She shook her head. Three chocolate drops stained his beautiful suit. "I'm not going anywhere with you."

"Fine." His expression hardened to granite. "Just answer one simple question before I go. Is the baby mine?"

A crazy sort of calm settled over her. She felt disconnected from her bedroom and from Sebastian. Chip had turned on her like this. She'd believed he cared about her. She'd trusted him and fifteen years later the pain remained fresh.

But her feelings for Sebastian weren't a teenage crush.

She loved him with everything in her and he'd accused her of something horrible.

"Yes," she whispered, a hollow shell waiting to be filled with agony. "The baby's yours. But after this, I'll never be."

...

Eleven

Missy's pronouncement droned in Sebastian's ears like a dirge as he drove to his parents' house. She'd never be his. That's where she was wrong. If she was pregnant with his child, she was going to find out that mere words would not get him to back off. He just needed a little time to regain control over his emotions.

Finding out that she was pregnant and that she'd intended to keep the truth from him roused every negative attitude he'd ever had about relationships. How many times had Chandra pulled some stunt when she wanted his attention? Too many to count.

But Missy wasn't his ex-wife. He'd been wrong to paint the two women with the same brush. Missy wouldn't deceive him into marrying her by passing another man's child off as his. No, quite the opposite. He wouldn't put it past her to lie to him in some misguided attempt to make things easier for him.

The child she carried was his. In his gut he'd known the truth before the question had surged out of him. He never should have let past mistakes ruin his future happiness.

Cursing, Sebastian stomped on the brakes and stopped inches from Max's car parked halfway up his parents' circular driveway. Distracted driving wasn't like him. But since that first night in Las Vegas, much of his behavior had become unrecognizable.

A collection of familiar cars were parked all around. The party was under way. He was one of the last to arrive. Sebastian listened to the engine cool, keenly aware of the empty passenger seat. This is not how he'd imagined the evening going.

Inside, his mother was the first to greet him.

"Happy birthday." He kissed her cheek and slipped her gift into her hand. "Sorry I'm late."

"Where's Missy?"

"She's not coming."

"Why not?"

Sebastian grimaced. "It's complicated."

"There you are." His father joined them in the foyer. "Where's your date?"

"Not coming." Sebastian had been too busy dwelling on his troubles with Missy to concoct a decent excuse for her absence.

"That's odd. When I spoke to her this afternoon, she was looking forward to it."

"She changed her mind," he said, hoping his bland tone would prevent further questions.

"That's not like Missy," his mother chimed in.

"Not at all," Brandon agreed. "What happened?"

"Nothing." Feeling ganged up on, Sebastian tried to turn the conversation away from him. "Looks like you have a houseful. Am I the last to arrive?"

"We're still waiting on Trent and Amy," Susan said, referring to her husband's brother and sister-in-law. "Come have a glass of champagne and say hello to everyone."

Sebastian would have followed his mother, but a hand on his arm stopped him. He glanced toward his father.

"Do you want me to call her and see if I can get her to come? Your mother was looking forward to having her here."

Irrationally irritated, Sebastian glared at his father. "A phone call from you isn't going to convince Missy to come tonight. She doesn't want to be here." With me. The last two words went unsaid, but Sebastian could hear them echoing in the foyer.

"You might be surprised how persuasive I can be. I got her to stay at Case Consolidated Holdings after you let her quit." Brandon leveled a disappointed look at his son. "I'd hoped if she stuck around long enough you might come to your senses. I can see I overestimated your intelligence."

"Come to my senses?" Sebastian repeated. "What the hell are you talking about?"

"She's in love with you. Has been for years." The older Case nodded knowingly.

His father's words hit him hard. "What?"

"And at long last, you're in love with her." Brandon waved his hand when Sebastian began to speak. "Don't bother denying it. It was all over your face that morning at the hotel."

"I have no idea what you're talking about." But he wasn't completely convinced he believed that. Something had happened between them that first night. "We were together, sure, but it was one night."

Brandon's smile turned sly. "And since?"

"That's none of your business."

"You were ornery and distracted when she was visiting her family. And since she's back, you've had a bounce in your step."

Sebastian couldn't believe what he was hearing. "I don't bounce."

"Well, you sure won't be if you let that girl get away. Smart, beautiful, funny. Good at getting things done. The office ran more smoothly once she came aboard. And she knew how to handle you." Brandon nodded, his expression self-satisfied. "I knew a week after she took the job that she was the best thing that ever happened to you."

And deep down, Sebastian knew it, too.

He rocked onto his toes, thrown off balance as his father clapped him on the back.

"That's my boy. Now, why don't you go fetch her? Give your mom a birthday present that'll really make her happy."

Sebastian thought about his child growing inside Missy and muttered, "I think I already have."

The drive from Missy's house to his parents' house had taken thirty minutes. The return trip seemed to take an eternity. While he negotiated Houston's traffic, he prepared a convincing argument for why she needed to forgive him. He parked in front of her condo and immediately saw her car was missing from her parking spot.

When she didn't answer her doorbell or respond when he knocked, he knew in the time it had taken him to come to his senses, she'd left. Next he tried her cell phone, but she wasn't picking up. Only one place made sense for her to have gone. Home.

And that's where he intended to follow.

The day after her big fight with Sebastian, Missy pulled into her father's driveway around ten in the morning. After he'd left, she'd been too upset to sit in her condo and rehash the mess she'd made of things. Instead, she'd taken a shower and headed for Crusade.

Three hours out of Houston, she'd decided to stop for the night. Her family wasn't expecting her until the next day, and when she'd fled Houston, she hadn't considered that her six-hour drive would put her at her father's house around one in the morning. Besides, after exhausting herself with anxiety and recriminations, she wasn't in any shape to drive that far in the middle of the day, much less at night.

Heart thumping too fast, she stared at the car parked in her father's driveway. Sebastian's Mercedes stuck out like a couture gown at a country dance. What was he doing here? She opened her door as family members poured out of the house. Sebastian led the way.

"Where have you been?" He jerked the car door from her hand, opening it wide, and dragged her from the seat. His hands explored her face, arms and shoulders. His gaze traced her forehead, cheeks and nose as if to reassure himself she was okay. "I left you a dozen messages. Why didn't you call?"

"Because I turned off my cell. A dozen messages?" Her traitorous heart danced for joy at his concern, but she pulled away from his touch. "What are you doing here?"

"When you didn't show up or call we all thought something had happened to you," Sebastian explained, cupping her face in his hands. "Where have you been?"

"I was tired so I stopped at a motel and slept." His somber, worried expression was beginning to blur the reasons why she'd left him in the first place. "How did you know I was coming here?"

"When I went back to your house last night and found you gone, I figured you'd head home."

"But why are you here?"

"I came to apologize."

"You're apologizing?" That didn't sound like Sebastian. What was the catch? "What if I'm not accepting?"

"Why wouldn't you?"

She looked around the tall man blocking her view of the group clustered in front of her car and spied her father standing behind him, a wide grin on his face. Her brothers and sisters-in-law were all standing too close for her to have this conversation with Sebastian.

"If you don't know, then there's no use in telling you."

Missy reached into the car and pulled out a duffel filled with clothes. To her annoyance, Sebastian plucked the bag from her hands and grasped her by the elbow.

"You obviously have something to get off your chest. Let's go inside and talk."

"No." She twisted her arm free. "No more talking. Look around you, Sebastian. This is where I'm from. My family doesn't have money or power. We have love. We have trust. We have each other's backs. And that's enough."

"I don't get what you mean."

"I don't care about your money or your fancy friends. Love. Trust. Commitment. That's what I want in a relationship."

Missy snagged her bag and strode into the house. She didn't realize that she'd left everyone outside until she reached the stairs to the second floor and the silence pressed in on her.

Turning, she peered through the front picture window and spotted Sebastian getting into David's truck. Where was he going with her brother? Her father entered the house.

"What is the matter with you?" he demanded. "That boy drove all night to get here and he's been fretting like a dog with fleas when you didn't show. Why are you acting like he's the enemy?"

For a second Missy didn't know how to react. Her father never scolded her. That had been her mother's job, and after the stroke stole her voice, her brothers' responsibility.

"I don't know why he came."

"He came because he loves you."

Her heart jerked. "Did he say that?"

"Not in so many words."

Not in any words.

"He's not in love with me," she said, flinching away from the stab of disappointment.

"Then why does he want to marry you?"

"He doesn't." A loud thump rang out as she sat down on the worn wood stairs. "What gave you a crazy idea like that?"

"He asked my permission."

Suddenly she couldn't breathe. "He did?" Who did that anymore? The traditional gesture was so sweet and so unlike Sebastian that Missy couldn't wrap her head around it. "Or is it just what you hope he'll do?"

"I'm not so addled that I don't know when a man's asking for my only daughter's hand in marriage." Her father sat beside her and took her hands in his, rubbing them to restore warmth. He smelled like soap and barbeque sauce. "In case you're wondering, I told him yes."

"I wish you wouldn't have done that."

Missy rested her head on his shoulder like she'd done as a child. Her father had always been her comfort zone when having four older brothers got to be too much for her to handle. Or when her mother tried to mold her into the polite, refined young lady a pastor and his wife could be proud of.

"It's done. Can't be undone. Is there a reason you don't want to marry him?"

She took a moment before answering. Sebastian's accusation had hurt. He'd shaken her trust in him and that wasn't something that could be repaired overnight. Besides, the original reason for avoiding a relationship with him hadn't changed.

"I don't fit into his world. He has money and lots of well-connected friends. I'm just a small-town girl who's been working as his assistant for four years. There's nothing sophisticated or interesting about me."

"So, you're afraid."

Her father had been counseling engaged couples for years. He'd probably seen it all. No use trying to deny the truth.

"Terrified."

"I don't know him well, but unlike that young man you dated in high school, Sebastian doesn't strike me as the sort who'd feed you to the wolves."

"No," Missy agreed. "You don't know him well. He's not

narrying me because he loves me." She puffed her breath out
n a huge sigh. "I'm pregnant."

Her father sat in silence for a long moment. When he
spoke, a deep sadness filled his voice. "Tim's?"

"No." She shook her head, the burn of tears blurring her
vision. "Sebastian's. That's why he wants to marry me. It's
why he married his first wife. He's honorable."

"Do you love him?"

"Yes. But I'm not going to let him make the same mistake
twice."

"I don't think he views marrying you as a mistake."

She twisted her hands in her father's grasp until she held
him. She squeezed gently, thinking of all the people he'd
touched both physically—with a gentle hug, a comforting
hand on the shoulder during a moment of grief—and with
his wise sermons and thoughtful counsel.

"He can be rather thick-headed that way."

Laugh lines deepened at the corners of her father's dark-
brown eyes. "I can see he's going to have a tough time convincing you to marry him."

"Tougher than you know. He's terrible at negotiating."

The front door opened and Matt's wife, Helen, entered, followed by David's very pregnant wife, Abigail. They carried
bowls and trays.

"What's going on?"

"It's Memorial Day weekend," Helen explained. "We're
barbecuing."

Missy got to her feet. "Do you want some help?"

"We've got it covered."

Abigail winked at Helen. "We wouldn't want you killing
Sebastian with your cooking."

Of all the household tasks Missy had mastered after
her mother's stroke, cooking was not one of them. And it
wasn't as if she got much time to practice. Sebastian kept her

working until seven most nights. She usually grabbed take-out on the way home.

She headed upstairs to drop off her duffel bag. Passing David's old room, she spied Sebastian's suitcase in the corner. He was staying here? In the room next to hers? How was she expected to get any sleep knowing he was on the other side of the wall?

Emotions churning, she sat on the window seat that over-looked the garden in the backyard. Her mother had planned and lovingly maintained each and every bed from the vegetables to the roses. After she'd had her stroke, Missy tended the garden while her mother looked on. At first Missy had resented the weeds that seemed to sprout overnight. The task of keeping the numerous beds in perfect order had pained her with its tedium.

Eventually, however, she began to find the repetitious chore soothed her restless nature. She'd read up on the various types of plants and dreamed that when she moved into her own house, she'd spend many free hours creating colorful plantings around her property.

"We're heading over to bring the boys some lunch. Want to come?"

Helen and Abigail hovered in the hallway.

"Sure." She snatched up the battered Stetson she wore only when in town and followed her sisters-in-law downstairs. "What are they doing today?"

"Repairs on the Taggets' roof," Helen said. "Last week's thunderstorm did quite a bit of damage to a dozen homes. It's been tough getting to everyone who needs help."

"Nice of your boss to pitch in," Abigail added. "Or should I call him your boyfriend?"

Missy pretended as if she hadn't heard the sly question. "Sebastian's working with them?" Is that why he'd been dressed in a T-shirt and jeans earlier? She'd been too agitated by his presence in Crusade to notice how he was dressed, but ow that she thought about it, she remembered he'd looked amned sexy in a snug cotton shirt that stretched across his hest and scarcely contained his biceps. "I didn't realize he vas handy."

"Apparently he worked construction during college," Helen aid.

How had she not known that? She'd worked for the man our years. And yet, how much had she discovered about him n the past couple of months? As much as he'd learned about er? Or had her determination to keep him at bay prevented im from getting to know her in turn?

Missy's pulse fluttered as Helen's SUV stopped in front of storm-battered house. More than just the roof had suffered rom the high winds. Half the front porch was missing and a ile of wood stacked next to a gaping hole in the front yard inted at a tree that was no more.

A dozen men swarmed the roof and yard. Missy had little rouble spotting Sebastian's tall form as he jumped off a adder and headed her way. She snatched her gaze from the vorn denim riding his narrow hips and wrapping his pow-rful thighs. She'd never seen him in jeans before and found he view disconcerting.

His expensive business suits gave him the air of an aloof nultimillionaire. Fascinating to look at but remote. The casual lothes made him much more approachable. Touchable. She vanted to hook her fingers into his belt loops and tug him lose enough for a long, slow kiss. Heat bloomed in her cheeks s he stopped beside her.

"Hello, Missy."

"Hi." Her mouth had gone too dry to offer more. The clean cent of sweat, soap and something uniquely Sebastian was so empting, she had to shove her hands into her back pockets to eep from reaching out to him. "Thanks for helping, but you lidn't need to."

He, too, wore a hat. The wide brim shadowed his eyes, forcing her to guess at his mood.

"I'm happy to pitch in."

"I didn't know you could handle a hammer."

"Figured me for a spoiled rich kid, didn't you?"

Missy hunched her shoulders. "Can you blame me?" Surrendering to temptation, she took his hand and turned it palm up so she could trace the lines and contours. She discovered rough spots she'd never thought about before, old calluses that revealed he hadn't spent his entire life behind a desk. "You don't have a workman's hands, but they're not exactly soft either." Not like Tim's hands. He'd never been one for physical labor.

"You'd better eat. We're only breaking for fifteen minutes." David held a sandwich in front of Sebastian's chest and gave Missy a meaningful look. "Why don't you get Sebastian a bottle of water?"

"Sure." Missy sent her brother a meaningful look of her own and released Sebastian's hand. When she returned a second later, her brothers had formed a crowd around Sebastian, blocking her from conversing with him.

Why were they keeping her and Sebastian apart? Was it to protect her or him? Watching the camaraderie between the five guys, she decided her brothers had come down on Sebastian's side. Resentment bubbled. Even they didn't think she was good enough for him.

And why was she so close to tears? Maybe it was because she agreed with them.

Twelve

Sebastian waited until Missy had driven away with her sisters-in-law before he returned to work. Repairing roofs hadn't been the plan when he'd trekked halfway across Texas; but, now that he was here, he remembered how much he enjoyed the satisfaction of a job well done.

The afternoon flew by. A pleasant ache entered his muscles as he and Missy's brothers accepted the homeowner's thanks and packed up the leftover materials.

"We really appreciate your help," Matt said, slamming the tailgate shut on his pickup.

David nodded. "Never would have gotten it done that fast without you."

"I enjoyed it." Sebastian joined Matt in the truck and leaned his arm on the open window. "How many more projects you got?"

"How many weeks can you stay?"

Sebastian laughed but gave the question serious consideration. How long had it been since he'd taken time away from the business to do something he enjoyed? Probably the last vacation had been his honeymoon. And he wouldn't exactly call that fun.

The truck sped through town as Matt headed back toward the parsonage. Sebastian removed his hat and let the wind dry the sweat from his brow and temples. He liked Missy's family. Discovering her father was a religious man had caught him off guard at first.

Why hadn't she ever told him about such an important part of her? What was there to hide about her family? From what he could see, there was nothing to be ashamed of. Each brother was happily married with kids. They had successful careers, good standing in the community.

What else didn't he know?

For four years she'd dressed and behaved in a manner he could only call conservative. Nothing flashy about her clothes or her lifestyle.

Then, in Las Vegas she'd unveiled a different side of herself he'd never dreamed existed. He loved both women. And now, after spending time with her family, he'd become that much more determined to keep her in his life.

Sebastian saluted Matt as he drove away. Hat in hand, he entered the house, eager to talk to Missy. Earlier, when she'd taken his hand and traced the lines on his palm, the simple touch had aroused so much more than his libido. If her brothers hadn't been standing nearby he'd have taken her in his arms and kissed her until she promised to love, honor and cherish him until death did they part.

Not that he was convinced that she'd have him after what he'd said to her.

The turn-of-the-century house contained an empty stillness as he entered. Wood floors creaked beneath his step as he headed for the back door. He paused in the kitchen for a glass of water and caught sight of Missy in the backyard, hoe in hand, tackling the weedy flowerbeds. He stepped onto the back porch to better admire the wiggle of her rear end in denim shorts as she dropped to hands and knees to attack the weeds crowded too close to the perennials to remove with the tool.

He released a sigh. The woman was flat out delightful no matter what angle she presented. Although he admitted a keen appreciation for the sight of her round backside thrust into the air. Grinning, he started down the steps for a closer look.

"You all done with the roof?" She straightened to a kneeling position and smudged her forehead with dirt as she wiped sweat from her brow.

How long had she been aware of him? Did she sense his nearness the same way he noticed hers? As if some invisible cord connected them to each other?

"We finished half an hour ago." He sat down beside her. "Looks like you have your work cut out for you."

"No one has time to keep it up since I left." She returned to her weeding. "Gardening was my mother's love. She designed and planted all these beds. After her stroke, she couldn't take care of them anymore so I took over." She attacked the invasive plants as if they personally offended her. "I used to hate working in the garden. It would take hours to weed even a single bed. The stupid things seemed to grow ten inches overnight. Mulching helps, but they still find a way in."

"Some things are like that, finding ways to thrive where they're not wanted." He longed to touch her, to get her to take down the wall she'd erected to keep him at bay.

"My mom was the most giving and kind person on the planet. Everyone loved her." She stabbed at the soil with her trowel, loosened a weed's roots from its hold, and flung it aside. The act seemed cathartic. As if she was ridding herself of stuff that bothered her. "She and I never got along. I suppose that makes me sound like a bad person."

She'd never talked about her mother except to say she'd had a stroke around the time Missy had turned fifteen and died almost ten years later.

"My dad and I don't, either," Sebastian said. "It's not unusual to get along better with one parent than another."

"My dad loved me unconditionally when I was growing up. It was my mom who was always trying to turn me into someone different."

"Different how?"

"Less tomboy, more young lady." Missy snorted. "I don't know why she expected me to act like a girl when all I wanted to do was run with my brothers and do everything they did." She drove the trowel into the dirt and sat back to dust off her knees. "See these scars? I got those jumping my bike off the ramp my brothers built in the parking lot behind the church. Busted my arm, too." She shook her head. "But do you think they got into trouble for daring me to try the jump? Nope. I got yelled at for doing something dangerous."

She wrapped her arms around her legs and set her chin on her knees. "Then there was the time when I almost drowned down by the lake because I dove off the dock and went in too steep and hit my head. That was my brothers' fault, but I got banned from the lake for the rest of the summer."

Sebastian couldn't stop a chuckle. "Sounds like you were lucky to survive childhood. I gotta admit, I never pegged you for a tomboy."

"I gave it up when I turned thirteen and figured out boys didn't date girls that could do more tricks on a bike or a skateboard than they could." Her grin came and went. "It was about that time that my mother really had her hands full with me."

He could see where she might have attracted a lot of male attention. "You were a little wild?"

"I was all about acting like that stereotypical daughter of a minister. You know, the one who behaves badly because life at home is so restrictive? I felt smothered by expectations of how I should behave, by how small the town was. My future stretched out in front of me like a west Texas highway. Empty.

flat and endless. Some days I thought I would explode if I didn't get out of here."

It wasn't a stretch to imagine her full of energy and frustration.

While Sebastian threw away the pile of weeds Missy had pulled, she gathered her gardening tools and put them away in the shed. They entered the house through the back door and headed upstairs to clean up for dinner.

"My dad told me what you asked him," Missy said as she reached her bedroom door. The way her remark came out of nowhere told Sebastian how much it had been on her mind. "It's nice of you to offer, and all, but I can't marry you."

"Any reason why not?"

"You're marrying me because I'm pregnant."

"In part." He cupped her face and held still until she met his gaze. "But that's not the only reason."

"No one expects you to do the right thing," she said, applying pressure to his chest.

"*I* expect me to do the right thing." He made sure she saw that he meant every word. "Besides, I don't want to stay a bachelor forever. I built my house with a family in mind. I want you and our baby to be that family."

She shook her head. "This is not the way I saw my future."

"How is it so different? In Las Vegas you resigned because you wanted a husband and children. You will soon have one. Why not the other?"

"Sure, but I never considered marrying you."

"Really?" Doubt and laughter tangled in his voice.

"Really." Her scowl told him she meant what she said.

"My dad thinks you're in love with me."

Her mouth popped open. Outrage brewed in her hazel eyes. "I won't deny having certain feelings," she said, her tone tart. "But even if I was madly in love with you, I'm not sure marriage between us is a good idea."

"If you were madly in love with me?" he teased. "You mean you're not?"

"It really doesn't matter if I am or not."

"It matters to me."

"They'll say I seduced you. That I got pregnant on purpose. I'm the one who's going to be looked at as a gold digger."

"No one will dare say anything to you." He kissed her long and slow to soothe her worries, keeping up the gentle pressure until she sagged against him. Only then did he release her lips and begin nibbling down her neck.

"Maybe not, but they'll be thinking it." She tipped her head to offer him better access. "I won't be accepted by anyone."

He never dreamed he would have to convince a woman that marrying him was a good idea. "That's nonsense."

"Is it? Up until five weeks ago, I was your executive assistant. Face it, Sebastian, I'm the last woman in Houston you'd have picked to marry."

Was she? If she'd said that before Las Vegas he might have agreed with her. Since then she'd become his obsession. "That's not true. Stop telling me all the things you think I need." His ex-wife had been shallow and showy. He'd sworn the next time he married it would be to a woman with depth and concern for more than herself. "You're warm, sensitive and real." He turned over her left hand and traced her lifeline the way she'd done earlier to him. "As much as I appreciate a glossy cover, what I can't get enough of is what's written on the pages between."

She tried to take her hand back, but Sebastian tightened his grip. Her lashes fluttered as he plied her palm with a soothing massage until her shoulders relaxed.

"I don't fit into your world."

"Stop saying that. I'm not your high school boyfriend."

"You accused me of seducing you to make you believe another man's child was yours."

"That was a stupid reaction to things that happened in my

past. I've regretted it every second since it happened. I swear I've learned my lesson. I'll never hurt you again."

"I want to believe you."

Her continued hesitation was scaring him. Sebastian knew it was time to pull out the big guns. "Maybe this will help."

He scooped something out of his pocket and slid it onto her ring finger. Against her dirty palm, the enormous diamond sparkled like a miniature star.

Groaning, Missy closed her fist, hiding the ring. "It's gorgeous."

"It's an Emma Case original," Sebastian said. "I had her design it especially for you."

"You had it designed for me?" Her resolve began to waver. Emma took weeks from design to execution. That meant that Sebastian had been thinking about proposing long before he found out she was pregnant. "Why are you doing this to me?"

"What?" His gray eyes were as dazzling as the diamond clutched in her palm. "Torturing you with expensive engagement rings and marriage proposals?"

"Yes, that."

"Because I don't want to live without you."

Hope surged in her. "You don't?"

"Of course not." He dusted her lips with his. "I love you."

"You do?" She didn't think she'd ever heard three more wonderful words.

A growl rumbled from his throat. "What do you think I've been saying?"

Missy bit back a flippant reply. She'd been wrong about so much. By not embracing her strength and not trusting Sebastian to keep her from harm, she'd nearly walked away from the love of her life.

"I love you." She launched herself against Sebastian's body, pressing her face against his chest. "I love you," she repeated, her declaration fierce and sure. "Marry me before I do something stupid."

Chuckling, he released the loose knot she'd bound her hair into. The strands rushed forward to consume his fingers as he framed her face and gazed down at her. Missy met his grin with one of her own as he lowered his head and kissed her.

Sebastian tugged her into the bathroom and got them out of their clothes. As hot water poured over them, his hands skimmed her body, his touch equal parts reverence and passion. Missy trembled beneath his gentle kisses, her blood heating to a quiet simmer as he toweled her dry.

"Your room or mine?" she quizzed, opening the door to the hall.

He came up behind her and slipped his arms around her. "Which room is closer?"

Voices filtered up the stairway toward them, followed by the thundering feet of excited children.

"You have way too many family members," he groused, dropping his chin onto her head. "Shall we get dressed and go tell them the good news?"

"You know my father and your mother are going to fight over where we should get married." She looked up at him. Her heart expanded as she realized this man was going to be hers for the rest of her life.

"That crossed my mind."

"What do you want to do?"

"I don't care as long as it happens sooner rather than later."

"I'm glad to hear you say that." She smiled. "Did you know it's only an eighteen-hour drive from Crusade to Las Vegas? If we leave now we could be there in time for lunch."

"Or, we could fly and be there in time for a late dinner." He nudged her inside her bedroom. "After we swing by a wedding chapel, of course."

"Of course." Missy grinned as he left her to go dress and pack.

* * *

Five hours later, Mr. and Mrs. Sebastian Case checked into the same hotel that had hosted the leadership summit. As they headed toward the elevators, Missy gazed with longing at the casino.

"We have a bridal suite waiting for us," Sebastian said.

"Just one spin of the wheel." She smiled at him. "For old time's sake? Please."

"One spin." Sebastian followed her to the roulette table and changed a hundred dollar bill for chips. "Black or red?"

Missy took the chips and put them on red. As the silver ball spun round, she leaned against Sebastian and for a second it was only them.

"Fifteen black," the dealer called.

"I lost?" She couldn't believe it.

"Lucky at cards, unlucky at love." Sebastian drew her away from the table. "Looks like your luck has changed."

"It has indeed," she said, snuggling against his side as they headed upstairs to start their honeymoon. "And I couldn't be happier."

* * * * *

MILLS & BOON®

Let us take you back in time with our Medieval Brides...

The Novice Bride – Carol Townend

The Dumont Bride – Terri Brisbin

The Lord's Forced Bride – Anne Herries

The Warrior's Princess Bride – Meriel Fuller

The Overlord's Bride – Margaret Moore

Templar Knight, Forbidden Bride – Lynna Banning

Order yours at
www.millsandboon.co.uk/medievalbrides

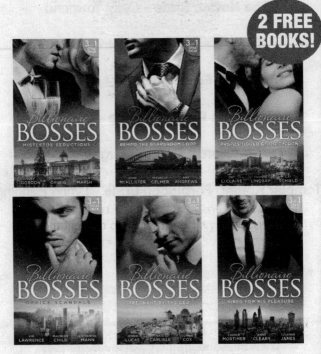

'The perfect Christmas read!' - Julia Williams

Jewellery designer Skylar loves living London, but when a surprise proposal goes wrong, she finds herself fleeing home to remote Puffin Island.

Burned by a terrible divorce, TV historian Alec is dazzled by Sky's beauty and so cynical that he assumes that's a bad thing! Luckily she's on the verge of getting engaged to someone else, so she won't be a constant source of temptation... but this Christmas, can Alec and Sky realise that they are what each other was looking for all along?

Order yours today at
www.millsandboon.co.uk

The World of
MILLS & BOON®

With eight paperback series to choose from, there's a Mills & Boon series perfect for you. So whether you're looking for glamorous seduction, Regency rakes or homespun heroes, we'll give you plenty of inspiration for your next read.

Cherish™

Experience the ultimate rush of falling in love.
12 new stories every month

Romantic Suspense INTRIGUE

A seductive combination of danger and desire
8 new stories every month

Desire™

Passionate and dramatic love stories
6 new stories every month

n o c t u r n e™

An exhilarating underworld of dark desires
2 new stories every month

For exclusive member offers go to
millsandboon.co.uk/subscribe

WORLD_ M&B2a